Yesu!

An Alternative Story of Life and Death of Jesus as it probably happened in Yoruba Land over two thousand years ago.

Yesu!

An Alternative Story of Life and Death of Jesus as it probably happened in Yoruba Land over two thousand years ago.

Abimbola Lagunju

Published by. Bersario Literary and Educational Services.

ISBN 978 – 978 – 989 – 042 - 2

For
Amelia Lagunju

Books by the same author

Days of Illusions
Cyclones of the Human Hearts
The Shadow of Rainbow
The Children of Signatures
The African in the Mirror
In the Embrace of Fear
Fouta Celebrates Life
Verses from Under The Sands
On the African Bus
Gombii and Other Short Stories
The Pelting March of The Storm (with Okey Nwayanwu)
Gadaffi's Gaffes
This Is Not Yet My Story

Foreword

Whenever we sing Hymn 438 in Yoruba in my Anglican Church, and we come to the chorus of the song that says: *"A! eje 'yebiye, T' o mu mi fun bi sno....."*, I always wonder what **sno** means in Yoruba. What will it mean to a rural Christian worshipper? How will a rural pastor explain **sno** to his congregation?

Then it occurred to me that indeed, there are many concepts, environments and words in the Christian Scripture that do not have any equivalent in Yoruba language or culture. We recite them, we memorize them and accept them as they are, without asking ourselves their meanings. This leaves the Yoruba reader, listener, singer of the events related in the scripture to interpret as he wishes, and to generate diverse mental images that may not necessarily correspond to the narrative in the scripture.

These thoughts led to the curiosity of how the story of the life of Jesus from his birth to his death over two thousand years ago would probably have played out in ancient Yoruba Land.

This is a work of fiction and does not in any way question or replace the contents of the Synoptic Gospels.

Abimbola Lagunju,
Ibadan, Nigeria
January 2021.

I

Yiofikun, seated on a mat on the floor beside his first wife Abike, called out to his second wife, Rojoyin, to bring him a keg of palm-wine. His day had been a long one. He had helped his neighbour thatch the roof of his house and installed the entrance door and wooden windows. He could not go today to his farm or inspect his traps, but he was very satisfied with helping out his neighbour. It was the way of life in their community, a picturesque village, called Betu-Akara perching on the banks of a big river, the River Monilo. In addition to being a roof thatcher, a farmer and a trapper, he also had a canoe which he rented out to neighbours to fish on the Monilo. He did not like water, his near-death experience at the river when he was a young boy permanently discouraged him from going near the river. He believed that his spirit and the spirit of the river were like water and oil that would never mix.

Like most of his neighbours, Yiofikun had two wives. They had no children. He was about 48 years old. His first wife, Abike, had been suffering from painful stiff joints which had kept her partially bedridden for the past few years.

Yiofikun, well-versed in traditional medicine had tried all the plants he knew and had consulted the local Babalawo to help Abike, all to no avail.

Rojoyin brought the keg of palm-wine; she knelt down to serve her husband. Yiofikun told her to sit beside Abike. He cleared his throat and said, "My dear wives, I have been intending to tell you something. It is an idea that I have been deliberating upon since Abike took ill." The two wives became very attentive. Yiofikun cleared his throat and continued, "It hurts me so much that Abike is in such pains that she can hardly take care of herself. And you, Rojoyin, I thank you very much for all the care and support that you have been giving your senior wife. You are a good woman. Olodumare will bless you and the children that you will soon have. I can see that you are overworked, always tired. Hmmnnn....I am thinking of taking another wife to help both of you out. What do you think?"

"Another wife?" Rojoyin asked. But I am not complaining. I am happy as we are now. I really do not want our husband to take another wife," she said.

"Abike, my mother, what is our husband talking about? Don't you think we are happy as we are?" She queried.

Yiofikun was fidgety. He remembered Abike's reaction when he announced sometime in the not-too-distant past that he wanted to marry Rojoyin. He looked at Abike for help.

"Be patient Rojoyin! Let us hear him out," Abike said. She turned to Yiofikun and said, "What exactly is the problem our husband? Tell us."

Yiofikun cleared his throat and said, "Two things worry me. Firstly, it is the workload on Rojoyin. She is the one that goes to the river to fetch water and firewood, she cleans the compound, she cooks the food, washes all our clothes and I feel that this workload was responsible for her last miscarriage. I would like for her to bear a child. Secondly, you both can see that I am not getting younger. I am the only married man in our clan without any children. I would like to have an heir. I am not saying that both of you will not bear children, but who knows, maybe the arrival of a new wife will change everyone's luck. Please understand that my suggestion to take another wife is not to spite you in any way."

Rojoyin was downcast.

Abike looked at Rojoyin, smiled and said, "Yiofikun, can you go out so we can discuss this please?" Yiofikun sighed, took his pot of palm-wine and walked out.

"Your husband wants another wife!" Rojoyin said. Abike laughed out loud and said, "He has made up his mind. Maybe we should look for one of our cousins for him to marry. I don't want him to bring just anyone into the house. Do you have any of your cousins in mind?"
Rojoyin shook her head and tearfully said, "They are all very young. Sara, who is eighteen years old just got married. Let us ask him if he has anyone in mind."
Abike said, "Let us ask him. Go and call him."

Yiofikun and his wives further discussed his intention and he acknowledged having seen a young girl of about eighteen years that he thought he could marry. She was the daughter of one of his friends in one distant village called Betu-Alafia. The father of the girl died a couple of years ago. The girl was living with her mother and her two sisters.

The wives agreed and it was decided that Rojoyin would accompany Yiofikun's uncles to the young girl's village to go and meet the parents and relatives of the maiden and ask for her hand. With Yiofikun's reputation as a very responsible and caring man, they knew the clan of the girl would assent to the marriage. They all agreed that in case Rojoyin didn't like the girl, then Yiofikun would have to look for another wife or abandon the idea completely.

A few days later, Rojoyin and two uncles of Yiofikun made the trip to Betu-Alafia, which was further inland away from the River Monilo. They met with the parents and relatives who were very happy to receive them. They knew Yiofikun very well and respected him. They felt very honoured that such a decent man had taken an interest in their daughter. They gave their consent conditional upon acceptance by the young maiden to marry Yiofikun.

They called her out to meet with Yiofikun's people. She stepped out of the doorway. A very beautiful girl with flawless, smooth velvety ebony skin. The white of her eyes were brilliant white. She was shy. She knelt to greet the visitors. Her parents informed her of the purpose of the visit of the strangers. She smiled and said, "whatever you, my parents think is best for me". Her name was Famurewa, but everyone called her Murewa. Rojoyin instantly liked her.
The mother and the visitors said prayers for her.

According to tradition, she was betrothed from that moment on. Her clan and the visitors agreed on the next steps that the tradition demanded.

A few weeks later, Rojoyin and three old women from Yiofikun's clan went again to Murewa's village. This next step of the tradition would determine the dowry that would be paid for Murewa's hand. As tradition demanded, only Murewa, her mother and old women from her clan would be present for this important visit. Food had been prepared for the visitors, but they could only eat after their mission and if the outcome was positive.

The women from both clans invited Murewa into one of the rooms. Their mission was to ascertain her virginity. If she was a virgin, a gong would be sounded to inform the whole village and a huge celebration would ensue. If she was not, then a talking drum would be beaten.

A few moments after the old women went in with Murewa, the gong was sounded. Women from adjoining compounds rushed into Murewa's parents' compound to celebrate. As tradition demanded, Murewa dressed up in a gorgeous attire and a beautiful headgear. Her face was veiled. She stepped into the compound to dance with the women. It was a graceful dance that many people still remember till today.

Rojoyin and her entourage returned happily to their village to relate to Yiofikun and his clan the outcome of their visit in order to begin preparations for the dowry ceremony.

Yiofikun set about preparing for the dowry which included thirty-three *orogbo (bitter kola)*, thirty-three kola nuts, five kegs of palm-wine, forty yams and two bags of salt as well as small measures of myrrh and frankincense. The myrrh and frankincense would be burnt during the dowry ceremony.

About a month later, the dowry was ready. About ten members of Yiofikun's clan including Rojoyin set out for Murewa's village for the ceremony. They were well received. There was a big celebration with a lot of dancing. The dowry was given to Murewa's clan. Murewa was very happy. The date of marriage which would hold in Yiofikun's house would be in four moons as tradition demanded.

II

Murewa's household transformed from a quiet environment into an open house from the day the dowry was paid. Women from her clan visited regularly to train Murewa in different aspects of being a wife. Her cooking and house-keeping skills were honed. She was specially trained in individual self-care to entice the husband.

One day, Murewa joined her younger sister and another woman from the village to go to the river to fetch water. A branch of River Monilo, from where the village sourced its water was about twenty minutes away. They left when the sun was high up in the sky. It was the first time Murewa would be going to the river since her betrothal. The women chatted and sang as they travelled the well-known route through the forest to the River. On seeing the River at a distance, the three young women raced towards it.

They sang as they fetched water from the River. "Murewa, show us how you will dance on that day," Murewa's sister said. "Oh yes! Show us!" The other woman enjoined. Happily, Murewa started dancing gracefully, singing,

"Ododo mi o, Ododo mi o, Ododo mi o"
"Elo ni o, elo ni o, ododo re o?"
"Iyebiye ni, iyebiye ni, ododo mi o"
"Iyawo mi o, iyawo mi o, iyawo mi o"
"Ololufe mi, ololufe mi, baba omo mi"
The girls joined her in the dance.

Done with their dancing, the women put their pots of water on their heads and started their return journey to the village. Murewa was a few paces in front of the other two women as they navigated the narrow footpath. The three women saw a tall man in billowing white robes, walking with a white staff coming slowly from the opposite direction. As he approached them, they could see that he had an unusually bright face. He looked old at one moment and young at the other moment. It seemed like he had two different faces. As Murewa was in front, she was the first to greet the man. With her pot on her head, she knelt down and greeted the man. The man responded in a deep guttural voice with a thick accent that was strange to Murewa and the other women. The man put his staff into his left hand and stretched his right hand to help Murewa up on her feet. As his hand touched Murewa, she felt a tingling sensation in her head which spread to her chest and seemed to settle in her belly. The man smiled at her and said, "you are blessed, my daughter."

The man continued on his journey and the women walked back towards their village. The women discussed the accent of the man and tried to identify its community of origin.

"The man looked strange to me," Murewa's sister said.

"And the face! I could not bear to look at the face," the other woman said.

"Oh yes! The face looked old and young at the same time. Did you notice how intently he looked at Murewa?" Murewa's sister asked.

Murewa did not tell the other women what she felt when the man helped her up from her knees. She did not tell them either how much she was feeling at peace within herself.

They soon forgot about the man and started teasing Murewa on her soon-to-be-wife status and how lucky she was to be marrying into Yiofikun's clan.

"Is Yiofikun tall or short? Is he fat?" the other woman asked Murewa.

Murewa smiled and said, "I have no idea, but he is very handsome anyway."

They all laughed as they walked into their compound.

III

A few weeks....

It was Murewa's mother that first noticed the changes in her daughter. Murewa slept longer than usual; she ate more and took short naps which was unusual. Her skin was a bit pale. There was one morning when she threw up. The mother was worried. She knew that Murewa had not met Yiofikun. Could she be pregnant? One morning, Murewa's mother called Murewa to her room.

"Murewa my daughter, I have noticed some changes lately in you. You sleep longer, you eat more, and you are gradually putting on weight. The other day, you vomited in the morning. Is there anything wrong with you?" Murewa's mother asked her gently.

"Mother, I have no idea. I feel tired sometimes, but that is all. But I have this strange feeling of peace in my body. I do not remember how it felt to be a child; but I think the way I feel is like the way a healthy baby feels," Murewa responded.

"Hmmmm….you have all the signs of pregnancy, Murewa!"

"Ah! Mother, this is not possible. I have not even met my husband-to-be. It has to be something else," Murewa said.

"When was the last time you saw the monthly visitor, I mean, your period?

"I have not seen it in the last two moons," Murewa said.

"Murewa! I think you are pregnant! Did any man in the village touch you?"

"No, Mother! You know I do not go out. Everybody knows that I am betrothed to Yiofikun. Please do not entertain such thoughts."

"This is trouble, this is a big shame to our family and our clan. Soon it will be evident to everyone that you are pregnant," Murewa's mother lamented. Murewa started to cry.

Soon all the women in the clan noticed the changes in Murewa, and they knew she was pregnant. They felt let down by Murewa and started avoiding the family.

IV

About a week before the marriage, Yiofikun asked Rojoyin and four clan women to visit Murewa in her village. He wanted to have news of her and her family. He prepared a lot of gifts to send to his new in-laws.

The women left early the next morning for Murewa's village. On the way, they saw a man in white billowing robes with a staff in his hand coming from the opposite direction. As he approached them, they could see that the face looked old in one moment and young at the other moment. They could not look into his dark intense eyes.

They greeted him politely and he answered them in a deep guttural voice with a thick accent that they could not identify. He opened his arms as he returned their greetings. The five women felt a tingling sensation in their heads. Simultaneously, they snapped back their heads and touched their right temples. The man, for unknown reasons, said, "Wisdom from the Most High!" He then asked them for direction to a nearby village which they explained to him. They continued on their journey towards Murewa's village.

On getting to Murewa's compound, they instantly observed how silent the compound was. There were no women going out or coming into Murewa's house. There was no cooking. It was strange. They murmured between each other before they approached the door.

They knocked on the door, and Murewa's mother opened it. They could see instantly that the woman had been crying. Her face looked swollen and they suspected that the woman had not been sleeping for days. They greeted her and set down the gifts that Yiofikun had sent to the family.
Murewa's mother brought out a mat which she laid under the tree in their compound. The women sat down. The visitors asked after Murewa. The mother said Murewa was sleeping but she would go and wake her up. She went into the house.

"Something is happening here," Rojoyin said.
"Yes, it all looks strange. They are supposed to be celebrating," one of the clan women said. They chatted on the situation and waited for Murewa to emerge from the house.

After a long wait, Murewa's mother emerged from the house with Murewa's sister tagging along carrying bowls of food. They set the food on the mat. Murewa's mother and the sister retuned to the house to get water.

"But this is strange! It is Murewa that is supposed to serve us, not the mother and the sister. We won't eat this food until we see Murewa," Rojoyin said. The other women agreed.

Murewa's mother soon emerged from the house carrying the pot of water. She sat on the mat with the visitors. The visitors thanked her and told her that they would not eat until they see Murewa.

Distraught, Murewa's mother went back into the house to call her daughter.

Soon after, Murewa emerged from the house with her mother.

The visitors could see from the distance that she was pregnant! They scrutinized her as she approached them. They could see she had also been crying.

Simultaneously, the women remembered what the man they had met on the way said, "Wisdom from the Most High!"

They got up from the mat, Rojoyin hugged Murewa and the other women encircled them. Murewa sobbed. Murewa's mother sobbed. Her younger sister was also crying.

Rojoyin took Murewa's hand and asked her to sit beside her.

"What happened Murewa?"

"I don't know. My mother said I am pregnant. I have not seen my monthly visitor for two moons," she sobbed.

"Don't cry, Murewa. Try to answer our questions truthfully," Rojoyin said.

"I don't tell lies. I will answer the questions."

"Have you had any relationship with any man?" the most senior woman from Yiofikun's clan asked.

"No. Never!" Murewa answered.

"And you said, you have not seen your monthly visitor for two moons?"

"Yes. It just stopped."

"This is a serious matter," the woman said.

"Murewa, go inside. We want to discuss the matter among ourselves," Rojoyin said.

Murewa's mother followed her daughter inside the house. They were both sobbing.

"This is a very strange matter! Never heard of such a thing. A young girl, who claims she had not related with any man is pregnant," Rojoyin said.

"Very, very strange," the other women chorused.

"What do we do now?" Rojoyin asked.

Again, the man's words "Wisdom from the Most High!" flashed through their minds.

For a moment, they were all silent, then Rojoyin, in a trance-like state, said, "I have an idea. Let us confirm again her virginity. At least that would take the doubts of her unchasteness from our minds".

The other women thought it was a very good idea. But this would have to be done in the presence of some old women from Murewa's clan.

One of the women went to knock the door to call Murewa and her mother. Rojoyin and the other women tuned their attention to Murewa's mother and asked her if the old women in their clan who verified Murewa's virginity the first time were close-by. Murewa's mother confirmed they were around. They asked her to go and ask the old women to come and meet with them.

Four old women from Murewa's clan wearing long faces arrived in the compound in the company of Murewa's mother. They all sat on the mat. Rojoyin told them how they had found Murewa pregnant and how Murewa claimed not to have had any contact with any man. The old women were downcast with shame. Rojoyin further informed them that while the final decision depended on Yiofikun, they needed to establish some facts to share with Yiofikun.

"We will do anything you say or want," the eldest of the old women from Murewa's clan said.

"Thank you. What we are proposing is that we reverify Murewa's virginity to confirm if she has known any man," Rojoyin said.

The old women were alarmed. Many thoughts raised through their minds. While they were still hesitating, Murewa stood up gaily and said she was ready for the test. They all went inside.

Soon after, they all trooped out with surprise on their faces. They were agitated.

"But she is still a virgin," Rojoyin said.

"I don't understand," one of the women from Yiofikun's clan exclaimed.

"This must be an act of Olodumare," the other said.

The women from Murewa's clan who had been downcast were relieved.

"This is strange. I have never heard of something like this in all my years," one of them said.

"We need to ask the men to consult Ifa on this matter," another said.

Rojoyin and the other women from Yiofikun's clan went back to the mat, ate their food and left.

V

Back in their village, Rojoyin and the other women related the events that happened in Murewa's Village to Yiofikun and Abike. She did not mention the man they had met on the way. She felt it was unimportant and was not related in any way to the issues at hand

Yiofikun was devastated. Abike cried.

Rojoyin emphasized that Murewa was still a virgin and that there were no signs that she had ever had any intimate relationship with a man. It was a mystery she said. They all agreed that Yiofikun would go early the next morning to the next village where Oluawo, the Ifa High Priest resided.

Yiofikun set out before daybreak to the Ifa High Priest's village. He was very troubled as he walked. This kind of story had never been heard of. He walked slowly, head bent, lost in his thoughts. He was not aware of the man coming in the opposite direction until he almost collided with him. The man wore billowing white robes. It was the same man that Murewa with her sister and her neighbour as well as Rojoyin and other clan women had met before. Yiofikun greeted the man and apologized to him for almost colliding with him. The man responded in his guttural voice and his accent.

"Master, you are not from this area, I suppose," Yiofikun asked.

"No, I am not. And I am not a Master, but a servant," the man said.

"Servant? You are dressed like a Noble, Master."

The man looked into Yiofikun's eyes, Yiofikun felt a shiver, and he heard the man say in the most guttural voice Yiofikun could imagine, ***"That which the Most High has entrusted unto you must be accepted, loved and protected. You are blessed among men."***

"Me!? I do not understand Master. I am just a simple servant of Olodumare, unworthy of his attention. Master, I am not aware of any new thing that God has entrusted unto me."

The man looked deeply into Yiofikun's eyes. Yiofikun was transfixed and he heard the man's voice like a gentle rumble of thunder repeat, ***"That which the Most High has entrusted unto you must be accepted, loved and protected. You are blessed among men."***

He heard himself in a voice that seemed to emanate from the totality of his being, like the rustle of dry leaves in the wind, say, "May the Will of Olodumare be done! Ashẹ Olodumare!

Yiofikun stood rooted in the same place for a few minutes and only came out of his trance, long after the man had gone. He rubbed his eyes, looked round and called out, but he was alone. He thought of what the man told him. He had no idea what Olodumare had entrusted unto him. He was troubled as he continued his journey to Oluawo's place.

Oluawo was outside in his compound when Yiofikun arrived. He greeted him and asked him inside. Oluawo looked curiously at Yiofikun as he took his seat. He gave Yiofikun three cowries in his right hand and asked him to close his eyes and concentrate on the cowries in his hands. After a few moments, the Oluawo told him to put the cowries directly on the *Opon Ifa (divination tray)*. Oluawo cast his *opele (divination chain)* on the *ọpọn ifa*. He moved the different parts of the sacred chain around the tray, then hailed Olodumare, saying,

Pápá nlá b'oju kugú
Ọrangun Ẹ̀kun,
A b'ọran pà à l'ẹ̀hin
ọpẹ nla b' ìdí yàkàtà
L'ó d'ifá fun Ódù

T'ó l'óun o ni i kú lailai
T'ó tún ní gbogbo árá
L' óun yó ó fi ya ọmọ
Ó ni óun ni àgbáàrà-gbá omi
Ti kò ni bèbè
Ti áṣẹ́ óun yio mà mu gbogbo ayé
O tun wa ni l'áṣẹ́ óun na ni a ma nwa s' ayé
Aṣẹ́ óun na ni ayé yio si ma j'àbọ̀ fun

He sighed and said, "Orunmila says, ***"That which the Most High has entrusted unto you must be accepted, loved and protected. You are blessed among men."***
Yiofikun was scared. It was the same message delivered by the man he had met on the way to Oluawo's place.

"What does this mean?" he asked Oluawo in a tremulous voice.

Oluawo shrugged and said that was the message from Orunmila to whatever question had brought him to his place. He advised Yiofikun to obey Olodumare without questions.

Suddenly, it dawned on Yiofikun as he sat in front of Oluawo that the message concerned the baby that Murewa was carrying. It was the handiwork of Olodumare! Olodumare through Murewa had come into his household in the form of man! Could this really be? If this were the case, then he was the most blessed of men. As he entertained these thoughts, Oluawo saw his demeanour change from dejection to surprise, then to happiness.

Yiofikun got up from the mat and thanked Oluawo for the consultation. He assured Oluawo that he would think about the message and wait to see whatever it meant. He took leave of Oluawo.

On the way back to his village, it occurred to him that he could go to Murewa's village to visit her and hear directly from her. He changed course and started towards Murewa's village.

VI

The sun was high up by the time Yiofikun arrived in Murewa's village. There was no one in Murewa's parents' compound. The place looked sombre, very quiet and looked like it had not been swept for several days. He stood in the middle of the compound and called out to announce his presence. After a while, Murewa's mother opened the door. She was so shocked to see Yiofikun that she quickly shut back the door. She assumed without any doubt that Yiofikun had come in person without his family to formally break up the engagement with Murewa. She broke into tears.

She covered her head with a shawl and was in tears as she opened the door and stepped into the compound to meet Yiofikun.
She greeted him and asked after his household.
Yiofikun replied and asked after everyone in the family. He did not mention Murewa, which added to the woman's anguish. She asked his permission to go back into the house to fetch the mat and a pot of water. Yiofikun nodded his assent and then added, "Please bring Murewa along." Murewa's mother again burst into tears as she nodded.

After a long moment, Murewa's mother emerged from the house with her daughter in tow. Murewa carried the mat and the pot of water. It was the first time Murewa was going to see her husband-to-be. As she approached him, she fainted and fell down. Strangely, the pot of water did not break and the water did not spill. Yiofikun ran to her and carried her up. He sprinkled some water on her face to revive her. He told her mother to spread the mat under the tree in the compound. He put Murewa on the mat. Soon Murewa opened her eyes and sat up. Yiofikun asked Murewa's mother to leave them, that he wanted to speak all alone with Murewa. The woman got up and went back dejectedly to the house.

Somehow, word had gone round the clan that Yiofikun was in Murewa's compound. As Murewa's mother went back to the house, she could see the clan women peeping from different angles at Murewa and Yiofikun sitting on the mat.

"Hello Murewa, how are you?" Yiofikun asked. Murewa was distraught. She looked at her hands as she wrung them. Tears were dropping from her eyes on her hands.
"Murewa, please be calm. Do not cry."
"I am pregnant!" Murewa blurted out and started wailing.
"I know that. Your senior wife, Rojoyin already told me. Please be calm. Tell me what happened and how it happened."
"I do not have any idea. It was my mother that first said that it looked like I was pregnant, and soon other women confirmed it."
Yiofikun was silent and looked into the distance. Then he asked, "Before people started observing

that you were pregnant, did anything strange happen to you?"

It was at that moment that Murewa remembered the encounter she and the other women had with the strange man on their way from the river. She narrated the encounter to Yiofikun and told him of the sensation that she felt as the man helped her up from her knees.

Yiofikun suddenly felt cold with fear. He gently asked Murewa to describe the man.

"He was a tall man. He wore billowing white robes. He walked with a white staff. He had an unusually bright face. He looked old at one moment and young at the other moment. It was like he had two different faces," Murewa said.

Yiofikun narrowed his eyes as it dawned on him that it was the same man that he had also met.

"Do you remember what he told you?"

"Yes! He said, "you are blessed, my daughter"," Murewa answered.

Yiofikun sighed deeply and said, "Murewa! Now I understand everything. I am going to tell you something, but you must promise never to tell anyone. It will be a secret between us forever."

Murewa nodded.

"I also met with the man on the way to Oluawo's place this morning. It was a very strange encounter. He told me that, that which Olodumare has entrusted unto me must be accepted, loved and protected. That I am blessed among all men." He also told her about his visit to Oluawo and that the Oluawo after divination also said the same thing. "Murewa! Olodumare has visited us through you. My heart rejoices!"

He stood up and helped Murewa up.

Murewa looked into his eyes, smiled, looked up to the sky. She stretched out her arms and said,

"Ọkàn mi yin Olúaye lógo,
Ẹ̀mí mi sì yọ̀ sí Ọlọ́run Olodumare.
Nítorí tí ó ṣijú wo ìwà ìrẹ̀lẹ̀ ọmọbìnrin ọ̀dọ̀ rẹ̀ lati orun wa:

Sá wò ó, láti ìsinsin yìí lọ gbogbo iran ènìyàn ni yóò máa pè mí ní alábùkún fún.

Nítorí ẹni tí ó ní agbára ti ṣe ohun tí ó tóbi fún mi;
Mímọ́ sì ni orúkọ rẹ̀.
Àánú rẹ̀ sì ń bẹ fún àwọn tí ó bẹ̀rù rẹ̀
láti ìrandíran.
Ó ti fi agbára hàn ní apá rẹ̀;
o ti tú àwọn onígbèéraga ká ní ìrònú ọkàn wọn.
Ó ti mú àwọn alágbára kúrò lórí ìtẹ́ wọn,
o sì gbé àwọn onírẹ̀lẹ̀ lékè.
Ó ti fi ohun tí ó dára kún àwọn tí ebi ń pa
ó sì rán àwọn ọlọ́rọ̀ padà ní òfo.
Ó ti ran Iran Yoruba ọmọ ọ̀dọ̀ rẹ̀ lọ́wọ́,
Ní ìrántí àánú rẹ̀;
sí Oduduwa àti àwọn iran rẹ̀ láéláé,
àti bí ó ti sọ fún àwọn baba wa."

Then she broke into a gracious dance as she sang,

"Yiofikun mi o, Yiofikun mi o, Yiofikun mi o
Ololufe mi, Ololufe mi, Yiofikun mi o"
Chorus*: Ododo mi o, ododo mi o, ododo mi*

Yiofikun responded, dancing and also singing,
"Murewa mi, Murewa mi, iyawo mi o
Mo ni fe re, mo ni fe re, iyawo mi o"
Chorus*: Ododo mi o, ododo mi o, ododo mi*

The clan women, Murewa's mother and sister watching from a safe distance emerged from their hiding places and joined in the dance.

Before he left the village in the evening, Yiofikun announced that the marriage would hold as planned in the next six days.

VII

Yiofikun arrived home very late. The moon was already high above. Abike and Rojoyin had been worried. They did not know what could have happened. They had been expecting Yiofikun at about noon. The village of Oluawo was not very distant. Rojoyin had cooked dinner but none of them had appetite to eat. They agreed they would wait for their husband to return before contemplating food.

"Don't you think we should inform one of his uncles? This is getting too late. I am worried," Rojoyin said.

"Let us wait a little moment more. It could be that there was some festival in Oluawo's village, and he decided to stay back to celebrate it with them," Abike responded.

"You think so? It is very much unlike him. He said he was going to be back before midday. I am getting worried," Rojoyin said.

"I understand you. This reminds me of one episode before he married you. He left home early in the morning to inspect his traps and said he would be back for breakfast. He did not return home until it was late. I was worried sick. Then late at night, I heard him come into the compound.

I was beside myself with anger. I asked him what happened. It turned out that one his friends in the next fell off a palm tree and he stayed back to treat him. It was a bad fall, and towards evening, the friend died. I knew that friend. My anger disappeared and I almost cried my eyes out. Then I started thinking about ghosts. Our husband specially hugged me that night." Abike said and winked to Rojoyin.

Rojoyin laughed and said "Abike, my mother! My turn to get that special hug this night!"
"He is all yours. These painful joints have taken my joy away." Abike said laughing.
"I am sorry Abike, my mother! Rojoyin said.
Abike painfully waved her off.

Soon, they had footsteps in the compound. Rojoyin hurried towards the door. It was Yiofikun. He looked happy. He greeted his wives and apologized for arriving late.
The wives were curious to know what happened; why he returned home so late. They wanted to know what Oluawo told him.

"Should we eat before I narrate what happened or do I narrate after food?" He asked his wives.

Both said they wanted to hear the story before food.

"Well, I went to Oluawo's place as I told you. He consulted Ifa and Ifa announced that I should take Murewa as my wife. Ifa said she was unblemished as Rojoyin had already reported and that the pregnancy was a mystery," he told his wives.

"And where have you been since then?" Abike asked.

"I went to Murewa's village to see her!" Yiofikun answered.

"What? You went there? What for?" Rojoyin asked.

"Yes! I wanted to reassure Murewa that the marriage would still hold in six days as planned. The poor girl and her mother were so miserable when I got there. But that has been settled. There was a little celebration in their compound, and I stayed back," Yiofikun explained.

"Hmmnn..! Yiofikun!" Abike murmured.

Rojoyin looked at Abike and said, "Hmmm! O ti fikun mi! Abike my mother! Our husband has totally fallen over! Do you think that what we discussed would work now?"

"Oh yes! He should be fined for going there all alone. You are awarded five straight nights."

"What are you women talking about?" Yiofikun asked.

The women laughed, then, Rojoyin said, "You will find out later. After dinner. Get some energy my husband!"

They all laughed. Rojoyin went to fix the dinner.

VIII

Six day later, it was marriage day.

As was the tradition, Murewa was bathed seven times by the women of her clan. She was scrubbed with seven different herbs and roots. Then her ebony skin was rubbed down with shea butter. Her palms and the soles of her feet were painted with *osun* (cam wood). Her hair was deeply rubbed with *adi eyan* (palm kernel oil) and then plaited into twelve cornrows.

Then, she was dressed in white and indigo *buba* (blouse) and a white *ofi* (woven material) wrapper. The *gele* (headgear) was *ofi* dyed in the purest indigo. She slipped on a pair of goat kid skin slippers. A white veil, covering her face was put on her head. From this moment on, no one except the husband could see her face this night.

Murewa stepped out of the preparation room into the compound. Tradition demanded that she sang and asked for blessings from her family before being escorted to her husband's village.

Sorrowfully, she sang:

Iya mo mi lo
E f'adura sin mi
Iya mo mi lo
E f'adura sin mi o

Ki nma m'osi, ki n'ma pade agbako n'ile oko
Iya mo mi lo
E f'adura sin mi o

Idile mo mi lo
E f'adura sin mi
Idile mo mi lo
E f'adura sin mi o

Ki nma m'osi, ki n'ma pade agbako n'ile oko
Idile mo mi lo
E f'adura sin mi o

In unison, as Murewa is being escorted out of her compound by the clan women, her clan and other guests stood up and sang:

Murewa o mi lo
A f'adura sin o
Murewa o mi lo
A f'adura sin o o

Ko ma m'osi, ko ma pade agbako n'ile oko

Murewa o mi lo
Murewa o mi lo
A f'adura sin o o

Murewa and her entourage set out for Yiofikun's village.

It was an uneventful journey.

IX

There in Yiofikun's village, the entire clan and their guests had been celebrating since morning. Many goats and chickens had been slaughtered and cooked. Bushmeat was in abundance. One of Yiofikun's friends had brought a freshly killed antelope. Freshly tapped palm-wine was in abundance. People sat on mats in the compound and ate and drank to their satisfaction. There was music. They all awaited the dusk when the bride would arrive.

As tradition demanded, the new bride must not meet the groom at home. The groom was expected to leave his compound to a friend's place prior to the arrival of the bride. In order to get early warning about, two young men would be posted to watch out for the arrival of the bridal train. Immediately the entourage is sighted, they would run back to the village to inform the groom, who would take his leave to his friend's place through another route. It was an abomination for the groom to meet the arriving entourage on the way. Later, the groom would return to his house through the same way that the bride had arrived in his compound.

According to tradition, ten young girls, five on each side would line the way into the compound to welcome the bride and ultimately the groom as he returns from his friend's place. The young girls would carry *fitilas* (earth lamps) to light the way into the groom's compound. They will accompany the groom back into the compound on arrival from his friend's place. They will go in front of the groom, singing to announce the arrival of the groom. Their *fitilas* must be kept burning. If perchance, the *fitila* of any of the girls should run out of oil and the fire dies, she will not be able to accompany the groom and cannot come into the groom's compound. It is almost an abomination that the *fitila* fire goes out. After the groom is back, no one else can come into the compound.

When the bride arrives with her entourage, women of the clan will welcome her into the compound. Water will be poured on the floor, and the bride has to step into the wet soil before she can enter the house.

As the clan and the guests celebrated in the compound, the sentinels ran in to announce that they had sighted Murewa's entourage. The young girls ran to the road with their *fitilas* and Yiofikun quietly left his compound for his friend's place. He knew the rules; it was his third marriage.

Soon Murewa's entourage arrived. Yiofikun's clan and guests burst into a song:

> *Kaabo, se daada lo de*
> *Murewa, aya wa,*
> *Kaabo, se daada lo de*
> *A ti nreti re,*
> *Kaabo, se daada lo de*
> *Si idile wa,*
> *Kaabo, se daada lo de*
> *Murewa, aya wa,*
> *Kaabo, se daada lo de*

As the clan sang, Rojoyin and other women of the clan poured water on Murewa's feet and on the ground. They escorted her into the house. The clan and their guests soon settled down. There were murmurs among the guests that it appeared the new bride was pregnant. "How could this have happened?" "How could Yiofikun have broken the tradition?" Some old women said, "We will see! If she is pregnant, we will know in a few moons. If she delivers before nine moons, then we will confirm our suspicion." The clan head who had been listening to the exchanges invited the clan council men aside for discussion.

"Do you really believe that this new wife is pregnant?" The old man asked the other men.

"She looks it. Didn't you see her belly?" Another responded.

"How could Yiofikun do this? This is an abomination. A shame to our clan," said the other.

The Clan Head shook his head ominously and said, "if she should deliver any child before nine moons, The Regulators must do their job. The child cannot and must not live among us. It must be banished from our midst." Everyone agreed.

Each clan in the community had a group of people they called Regulators, whose duty is to ensure that tradition is not broken by anyone. Their sentences for any breach of tradition after investigations were either death or banishment, which for many ultimately resulted in death.

Anyone, including children could be subjected to these harsh sentences. A child out of proper wedlock, a child with severe birth abnormalities can be banished. This banishment means that the child is taken far away from the village and left in the forest. The only revered child is an albino child, who is considered a messenger from the gods. The sentences were binding and lifelong. All members of the community were under obligation to ensure that the punishment was carried out.

While they were discussing, Yiofikun, escorted by the ten young girls with their *fitilas* arrived in the compound. The clan and the guests burst into singing and dancing:

> *Oko Iyawo,*
> *Kaabo, se daada lo de*
> *A ti nreti re,*
> *Kaabo, se daada lo de*
> *Oko Iyawo,*
> *Kaabo, se daada lo de*
> *Murewa nreti re*
> *Kaabo, se daada lo de*

Yiofikun took a few dance steps and then went into his house to meet his new wife.
The party in his compound continued under the full moon till about midnight.

X

Peace reigned in Yiofikun's household. Abike and Rojoyin showered love and attention on Murewa. She was not allowed to go to the river to fetch water or to the bush to fetch firewood. However, she cooked all the meals and washed the dishes. In the evenings, Abike entertained them with stories of the younger days of their husband. Being pregnant, Murewa slept in Abike's room and Rojoyin, to her pleasure had their husband to herself. She slept in Yiofikun's room.

As days rolled by, Murewa's baby bump became more visible. Her dark skin radiated. Everyone in the household was looking forward to the arrival of the baby.

Exactly six moons after the marriage, Murewa fell into labour one night. Abike and Rojoyin, having never had any children of their own were confused and did not know what to do. They woke Yiofikun up to tell him. He quickly put on his clothes, and with Rojoyin, they decided to take Murewa to the next village where an old woman that attended to births resided. They immediately set out, and as they walked, Murewa's labour pains intensified.

Murewa could no longer walk. The water broke. Yiofikun told Rojoyin to run to the village to bring the old woman. He looked for a clearing in the bush where Murewa could rest. There was a big iroko tree nearby. He gently urged Murewa to the tree, so Murewa could sit and lean against the tree. The sky was very clear and there were no clouds. The moon was full, and it appeared as if the stars shone brighter that night. There was a very gentle breeze that cooled the warm evening.

It turned out that the big Iroko tree was a shelter for goats and sheep of the village which the owners allowed to roam about freely. Fooled by the sun, some of the animals grazed nearby while the others squatted under the tree chewing cud.

The animals moved off as Yiofikun and Murewa approached the tree. They looked curiously at the pair. Yiofikun removed his agbada (a flowing garb) and spread it under the tree. He helped Murewa to sit down. The labour pains intensified. Yiofikun was beside himself with worry. He told Murewa that he would go back to the footpath to see if Rojoyin was on her way with the old woman.

He had just got the footpath when he heard the cry of a baby from Murewa's direction. He ran back to the Iroko tree and found Murewa with a baby in her hands. Murewa had wrapped the new-born with her *gele* and was carrying it in her hands. Yiofikun took the baby from Murewa's hand and checked the sex. He was very happy to see that it was a baby boy. He held him up to the sky and thanked Olodumare for the gift. Murewa was tired; she laid down to rest and Yiofikun put the child beside her to suckle. He sat beside his wife and soon they all dozed off.

It was Murewa that first woke up to the sound of people walking towards them. She nudged Yiofikun to tell him. As their eyes grew accustomed to the night, they saw the man in billowing white robes with a white staff. They both immediately recognized him. Murewa was scared. She thought the man had come to take away her baby. Yiofikun quickly got up to face the man. Then, they realized that the man was not alone. There were two other men, dressed in the same way behind him. The man stretched out his right hand and said, "Peace!"

The three men moved towards them and knelt and bowed down before the child. They said, "The

First and Only of Olodumare, you are welcome! We worship you!" The one that appeared to be the youngest among them then added, "I, your servant, have been assigned to watch over you for as long as your short journey and mission last. I, only visible to you, will always be with you to serve you my Master!"

While still on their knees, they dipped their hands in their white pouches and took out gifts for the child. One gave the child one old palm kernel and said, "This is as hard as rock. But it will sprout into a beautiful plant when watered with blood." The second man offered his gift too: thirty-three pieces of *orogbo*. He said, "Bitter thirty-three!" The third man also offered his gift. It was a pack of incense. He said, "As no one can hold smoke; and no one can live without air, your fame shall spread all over the world like sweet-scented air!" The three chorused "Peace be unto you!" and moved in the opposite direction from where they had come.

Soon after their departure, Rojoyin arrived with the old woman. She had come late because the woman had gone to a neighbouring village to visit her son. Rojoyin said she ran all the way to the village to find the woman.

The old woman returned to her house and Rojoyin sat beside Murewa and Yiofikun under the Iroko tree. The goats squatted around them, chewing their cud as they watched the family.

They left just before daylight for their home.

XI

Back in the house, Abike was worried. She had not been able to sleep since Murewa was accompanied by Rojoyin and Yiofikun to the next village. Her joints ached her severely. As she heard movements in their compound, she struggled to sit up against the wall in her room. Rojoyin was the first to enter the house to joyfully announce the delivery of a baby boy. Soon Murewa came in, followed by Yiofikun. Abike congratulated Murewa and painfully stretched out her arms to carry the new-born. As soon as the baby rested in her arms, Abike felt a strange sensation, like a draught of cold air over her body. Her body shivered and she felt all the aches and pains of many years that had kept her bedridden leave her body. She shouted! Everyone was startled and scared. She passed the baby to Rojoyin and stood up! She jumped up, she ran across the room and took some dance steps.

"What!?" exclaimed Yiofikun, rubbing his eyes.

"Mother!" Rojoyin and Murewa shouted.

Rojoyin gave the baby to Yiofikun and the two women ran to hug Abike. They danced around the room.

"All the aches and pains have gone! I feel whole like a new-born!" Abike repeatedly shouted.

She added, "I can now go to the river to fetch water, I can cook, I can do whatever pleases me."

Then, she came to where Yiofikun was seated with the baby in his arms. She knelt and bowed her head to the ground and said, "Thank you my Lord for healing me of my infirmities and making me whole again."

While still on her knees, she stretched out her arms again to carry the new-born. She held up the boy and said,

> "Olùbùkún ni Olodumare Obangiji;
> nítorí tí ó ti bojú wò, tí ó sì ti dá àwọn ènìyàn rẹ̀ nídè,
> Ó sì ti gbé ìwo ìgbàlà sókè fún wa
> Pé, a ó gbà wá là lọ́wọ́
> àwọn ọ̀tá wa àti lọ́wọ́ àwọn tí ó kóríira wá
> kí àwa kí ó lè máa sìn láìfọ̀yà,

*ni ìwà mímọ́ àti ní òdodo níwájú rẹ̀, ní ọjọ́ ayé wa
gbogbo.*

> *"Àti ìwọ, ọmọ mi,
> ọmọ Ọ̀gá-ògo jùlọ ni a ó máa pè ọ́!
> Láti fi ìmọ̀ ìgbàlà fún àwọn ènìyàn rẹ̀
> fún ìmúkúrò ẹ̀ṣẹ̀ wọn,
> nítorí ìyọ́nú Ọlọ́run wà;
> nípa èyí tí ìlà-oòrùn láti òkè wá bojú wò wá,
> Láti fi ìmọ́lẹ̀ fún àwọn tí ó jókòó ní
> òkùnkùn àti ní òjìji ikú,
> àti láti fi ẹsẹ̀ wa lé ọ̀nà àlàáfìà."*

Abike gave the child back to Murewa and turned
to Rojoyin and said, "Rojoyin, stay with Murewa,
I am going to fetch water from the river. After
that, I will go and fetch firewood. Then, I will boil
water and give Murewa and our child a very hot
bath. Then I will cook for everyone! This is the
best day of my life!"

Rojoyin wanted to protest but Abike was out of
the house before she could say anything.

Yiofikun told them that he had to go to inform the
members of his clan of the arrival of the new-born.

XII

Abike went to the river with two big pots to fetch water. Women in the village, who knew she had been bedridden for many years were very surprised to see her at the river. They greeted her warily, unsure if she was the one or an identical younger sister or an apparition of her dead self. She looked younger with no signs of pains or discomfort. Apparitions have been known to appear in the morning near water sources to mingle with the living. The women were scared. As they moved away from her, one woman said, "Abike, wife of Yiofikun, the *iyaale* of Rojoyin and Murewa, are you the one or your apparition?"

"I am the one! Why are you moving away from me? I am not an apparition" Abike said.

One other woman said, "She can't possibly be the one! This woman her looks younger than the Abike that we know! This is an apparition! Let us pour sand on her, so she won't disappear!"

As if being propelled by some force, the women picked up sand and poured on Abike, who burst out laughing.

The women moved closer to her. "We can see your aches and pains have gone. You look younger and more beautiful. What happened? Tell us," they chorused.

"It is the handiwork of Olodumare!"

"Really? Which Babalawo treated you?" one woman asked.

"No Babalawo treated me!"

"Then tell us what happened." They chorused again.

"Hmmm….I was healed this morning"

"Healed? Who healed you? How?"

"Hmmnnn….you know my new *iyawo (wife)*? Murewa?

"Of course. We were all at the marriage six moons ago! What has that got to do with your new state?" they asked.

"Murewa delivered a baby boy last night!" Abike said.

"What! An abomination! The Regulators must not hear of this!"

"This is not about Regulators. The child is a special child."

"How? Tell us the full story please!"

"Well, I asked to carry the child in my arms. I knew my joints would ache, but I wanted to carry him and welcome him to our household. Just a few moments after he was in my arms, I felt a cold shiver, and I felt all the pains, discomfort, aches and swollen joints leave my body like a little rustle of leaves! I felt good in my body and I stood up. No pains, no aches and no swollen joints," Abike confessed.

"Ahh! *Abami omo*! That's an *abami* child, a strange child!" one of the women said.

"You mean this child can cure any illness?" another woman asked.

"I do not know but see me! I am whole, health and full of energy after many years of being bedridden," Abike answered.

One woman said, "I am taking Orojakin, my blind husband to your compound right away! He has been blind since a snake spat in his eyes many years ago." She abandoned her pot and ran back to the village. The other women also abandoned their pots and ran towards the village.

Abike smiled. She quietly filled her pots with water. She balanced one pot on her head and left the river. She remembered what one of the women had said about Regulators and her heart constricted. She remembered one of the women calling the new-born *abami* child. She had to speak with Yiofikun about this, she thought.

She heard voices of people as she approached her compound. She hurried her steps to see what the noise was all about. She was astonished to see many people in her compound. All the women who had been at the river and others were there. They had brought many gifts for the new-born. But they had also brought their relatives inflicted with one illness or the other. The blind man was there; there were many with guinea-worm, some with elephantiasis, deaf and dumb and she recognized her childhood friend, Dansi, who since their teenage years had been suffering from haemorrhage. She had aged and looked very frail. Abike greeted her. She pulled Abike to the side and asked her, "Is it true that it was the child that healed you?" Abike nodded and said, "Yes, just this morning."

"You have to help me Abike. I need to carry the child in my arms," Dansi pleaded.

"I will see what I can do, but you understand that it will be difficult and dangerous to carry out the children among this mob," Abike said.

Abike went into the house.

Murewa was still sleeping, the baby lying by her side.

Yiofikun had not yet returned from the visit to the members of the clan.

Rojoyin had been awakened by the noise outside and asked Abike what was happening outside.

Abike narrated what happened at the river to her. They agreed to wait until Yiofikun came back. He would know what to do. Rojoyin went back to her sleep.

Abike quietly returned to Murewa's room to collect her dirty clothes as well as the cloth with which the new-born was wrapped after birth to wash. She also went into Rojoyin's room to collect her dirty clothes. When she stepped out to go and wash the clothes, she saw that more people had arrived. They had spread their mats on the floor and were waiting patiently. Abike told them that the baby and his mother were sleeping and asked them not to make noise.

She put the pile of clothes to wash on the floor, got water and soap and set to her task.
Dansi approached her friend and offered to help her wash some of the clothes. Abike was reluctant, but after some persuasion she accepted her friend's offer. They sat down to start washing. Dansi pulled the pile of clothes to herself. She chose one to put in the wash basin. It was the cloth with which the new-born was wrapped after birth. As soon as she touched the cloth, her body shivered, and she heard a faint sound like the rustle of dry leaves blowing away from her body.

"I am healed!" She shouted at the top of her voice. She jumped up from her seat and again shouted, "I am healed!"

Abike immediately knew that it was the cloth with which the child was wrapped that did the miracle. She immediately took the cloth out of the water and help it under her armpit.

The people seated in the compound rushed towards the two women. Dansi was beside herself. She pointed to the water in which she had put the cloth and pointed to the cloth folded under Abike's armpit. As the crowd surged forward to take the cloth from Abike, she held up her hand and screamed, "Stop there! Everyone will have his chance! Please make a straight line." The crowd scrambled into a straight line. She then took the cloth and soaked it in each of the two pots of water in the compound. Then she took a small calabash to decant small quantities of water for each person to drink.

The first person to drink the water was Orojakin, the blind man. His eyes blinded many years ago by the spit of a snake on his farm cleared immediately. He shouted for joy and ran round the compound. His wife and daughter, who had been saddled with leading him around followed in suit. As Abike dosed out the water to the afflicted, shouts of joy echoed in the compound. When the last person had been attended to, Abike took the cloth and marched proudly into the house. She found Murewa and Rojoyin peeping from a hole in the window to see the pandemonium outside. She told them what had happened. She was very excited.

Murewa, unsure of what all these events meant just smiled and did not take part in the excited exchange between Abike and Rojoyin. The three women took turns carrying the child until their husband returned.

XIII

It was almost dusk by the time Yiofikun returned home.

Abike and Rojoyin, with little participation from Murewa, narrated the events of the day to him. They were particularly excited with the fame the child had brought to the family. Yiofikun was surprised and worried. He knew that the case of the child, born six months after marriage and now seemingly doing some strange things, albeit indirectly would attract the attention of The Regulators. He called Abike and invited her into the compound for discussion. He wanted to know more about how it all happened.

Abike faithfully narrated the event of the day, from her trip to the river, the discussions with the women at the river who were surprised to see her and how she accidentally discovered the healing power in the cloth of the baby. She also told Yiofikun how one woman at the river had mentioned The Regulators and how another woman referred to the new-born as an *Abami* child.

"I am sure some of those people who were here this morning would have reported the case to The Regulators," Yiofikun remarked despondently.
"I did not have any bad intentions, Yiofikun. I am so sorry," Abike said dejectedly.
"It is not your fault Abike. Anyone would have done what you did. One cannot cover the brightness of the sun with a hand, that is the destiny of the boy: to be known!" Yiofikun said.
"And The Regulators? How are we going to manage them?" Abike asked, her voice tremulous.

"That is my concern. I think they will probably make a move soon. But I suspect they will not do anything until the boy is circumcised in seven days' time as our tradition demands. After that will be dangerous," Yiofikun responded.

"Hmmm… I don't understand our people. Practically all the people with infirmities and illnesses were healed in our compound today. The wives of two Regulators were here and some of the relatives of the others were here too. Do you really think they will want to hurt our boy after all the good they benefitted today and that which they stand to benefit?" Abike asked.

"That is the way of humans. They do not appreciate *good* until the *good* has left their midst. Don't you remember the story of *Orunmila* and *Olowo* his son and the people? Let us wait and see what will happen," Yiofikun said.

While they were in the compound, one of Yiofikun's cousins, Tanfẹ emerged from the darkness into their compound. He looked worried and was breathing hard. It was apparent he had been running.

"Tanfẹ, what is the problem? You look worried," Yiofikun inquired.

"I must not be seen here. Let's move further into darkness,"

"Tell us what the problem is," Yiofikun said as he led the way into a darker part of the compound.

"Yiofikun! You must leave the village with your family as soon as possible,"

"Why? *Kilode*?" Yiofikun and Abike asked simultaneously.

"They want to kill him! They plan to banish him!" Tanfẹ exclaimed breathlessly.

"Kill who? Banish who?" Yiofikun asked.

"Your baby, the *Abami* boy. I overheard them saying they will ask you to bring him over tomorrow night to their council," Tanfẹ said, and without another word, ran away from the compound.

Abike dejectedly sat on a stone in the compound, held her head and started crying silently. Yiofikun paced the compound in deep thoughts and later squatted beside Abike.

"We must leave this night," Abike said.

"We? You and Rojoyin do not have to go. I can leave with Murewa and the boy," Yiofikun offered.

"Never! We will all go together. We are one family. What will Rojoyin and I be doing here after you have gone? Don't you understand that we will be like outcasts and we will be mocked by everyone for running away from the sentence passed by The Regulators? We are all going together," she said.

Yiofikun thought for a moment, then said, "You are right. But we will leave very early tomorrow morning before daybreak."

They went back into the house. Yiofikun informed Murewa and Rojoyin of the situation and the need to leave the village in order to protect the little boy from The Regulators. Both women broke into tears.

XIV

The moon was still high up early the next morning when they quietly left their village. Abike carried the baby on her back, while Rojoyin and Murewa carried their belongings on their heads. Yiofikun whispered to them not to look back as they marched out in a single file. He led the way quietly out of the village towards the River Monilo. Abike and Rojoyin were surprised that they were going towards the River. They knew their husband had a phobia of any big body of water. "Where are we going?" Abike whispered to Yiofikun. She took a sharp breath when she saw his face, which seemed to have changed. The person leading them towards the River did not look like their husband. She wanted to cry out, but she could not. She thought of running away, but she felt as if she was being propelled by some external force in the direction of the River.

They soon arrived at the banks of the great River. Yiofikun led the group along the banks until they reached a big tree that cast its huge shadow on the River. Under the shadow was a long canoe and there was a man in white attire holding two long oars sitting at the helm of it. He did not look back as Yiofikun led his entourage to board the canoe. The man moved the canoe and steered it towards the centre of the River and began to row upstream. As the day broke, Yiofikun realised that the canoe sped eastwards. The sun was in their face for the duration of their trip.

About midday when the sun was high up, the man began steering the canoe towards the shore. He expertly docked the canoe under another big tree.

None of the passengers saw his face during the entire journey. Yiofikun stepped out and helped his wives out of the canoe. The canoe man moved off again to the middle of the River and continued to sail upstream.

The entourage continued their journey through the bush with Yiofikun in front. They observed that the vegetation was sparse, and the soil was dry and sandy. It was very different from their own environment. They found a bush path which they followed. Abike asked Yiofikun if he had any idea where the bush path led to. Yiofikun answered, "Olodumare, who has by his mercies led us to this place will guide us and lead us to our new abode."

Soon, the baby started crying. They stopped and Yiofikun got a clearing off the bush path for them to rest and for Murewa to nurse the baby. They all sat on the floor as Murewa attended to her baby. Satiated, the baby soon slept off. Rojoyin offered to carry the child on her back. While they were preparing to leave the clearing and retake the footpath, they heard a woman singing and coming along the footpath from the same direction from which they had been coming. They waited.

Soon the woman emerged with a pot of water on her head. She was scared when she saw them. She knew they were foreigners from the way they were dressed. She was about the same age as Murewa. She greeted them in her language and was pleasantly surprised, when the youngest woman in the entourage, Murewa, replied her. The woman and Murewa had some rapid exchanges while Yiofikun and his other two wives looked on in amazement. Murewa smiled as she informed the others that the woman's name was Efunyonda, but everyone called her Yonda, and that the next village, her village was called Betu-Ifẹ. Yonda had told Murewa that her parents would be happy to receive them in their house. She said her parents had always been expecting strangers for a very long time as Ifa had foretold. While not sure if they were the ones, she invited them along for her parents to judge.

They followed Yonda to Betu-Ifẹ. Murewa and Yonda chatted all the way to the village. Murewa learnt that Yonda was the only child of the family and had not yet married. She told Murewa that she was yet to marry, not because there were no suitors, but there was a boy she had set her eyes upon but who was just too shy. "And see, I cannot go to ask him for his hand!" Yonda said. Both girls laughed out loud.

Betu-Ifẹ was a village with many mud houses scattered between the sparse vegetation. The houses were well laid out. There were wide footpaths that could take twenty to thirty people walking side by side. Each house had a front yard demarcated by short dry-looking plants bearing red and yellow flowers. The compounds were very clean. The houses were of different sizes – some small, some quite big. All had carved wooden doors and windows. The village was very beautiful. Rojoyin whispered to Abike, "My mother, are we on this earth or in the land of the dead? This place is very beautiful."

Yonda marched them on to her house. She entered the front yard of a big house. As they entered, the door to the house opened and the parents of Yonda appeared. They stepped out and on sighting the baby sleeping at Rojoyin's back, they knelt and bowed their heads to the ground. Yonda's father said,

"Olúwa Olódùmarè, Oluaye!
Nígbà yìí ni ó tó jọwọ́ ọmọ ọ̀dọ̀ rẹ lọ́wọ́ lọ,
ní Àlàáfìà, gẹ́gẹ́ bí ọ̀rọ̀ rẹ:
Nítorí tí ojú mi ti rí ìgbàlà rẹ ná,

Murewa looked at Yonda; Yiofikun looked at his two wives, lost for words. Yonda's father further said, "We have been waiting for my Lord for a very long time. Welcome my Lord to our humble home, your home." Yonda's parents ushered them into their house.

XV

Back in Betu-Akara, Yiofikun's village, it was mayhem when it was reported to The Regulators that Yiofikun had escaped with his family. Many people, some of whom had come the previous day to see healing were gathered in Yiofikun's compound. Some shouted, "Death to the *Abami* child,", "An *Abami* child must not live among us!". Some threw stones at Yiofikun's house.

One woman asked, "Did anyone see the child?"

A small crowd gathered immediately around her.

"I do not think anyone saw the child. We heard of the child, but no one saw it," a woman offered.

"Is it a baby boy or a baby girl?"

"I heard it was a baby boy. Very dark-skinned like an adult," another said.

"I cannot believe that they could just escape like that. And no one saw them leave the village!"

"I would have followed them if Abike had told me," Dansi said.

"Shior! To do what?"

"To serve the child! I will give my life to defend the child," Dansi answered.

"Hmm…, she is planning to be Yiofikun's fourth wife," said another woman. The remark drew loud laughter from the small group of women. Dansi left the group embarrassed as their laughter followed her.

Suddenly everyone fell silent as a group of five men marched into the compound. They were the very rarely seen Regulators. They were fully dressed in black and their faces were painted in charcoal. Their arms were folded across their chests as they filed to the centre of Yiofikun's compound. They stopped and stood in a circle when they reached the centre of the compound. Many of the women who had been chattering before their arrival ran away when Regulators arrived.

There was a sixth man, called *Atokun* with The Regulators. His role was to attentively listen to the low tones of The Regulators and to announce their judgement. The Regulators did not directly address the public and they spoke in barely audible low tones.

There was absolute silence as The Regulators deliberated among themselves.

The *Atokun* cleared his throat and announced that The Regulators had ordered an immediate search party to go into the bush and surrounding villages to look for the family. Their mission was to bring the new-born alive back to The Regulators for sentencing. The hunters were instructed to forcefully take the baby from its mother. The parents were to be instructed not to come with the search party. Kiisa, the chief hunter of the village was assigned to lead the search party of other six hunters.

The Regulators filed out of the compound as silently as they had come.

Kiisa and the other six hunters heavily dressed in their traditional hunting gear left the village on their mission immediately. They had no idea which direction the family could have taken out of the village. They looked for their footprints or any telltale signs, but they could not find any. They decided to move into the bush and do a search. Kiisa assigned directions to the hunters and told them to either shout or blow their horns if they sighted the family or their trails. The hunters went in different directions assigned to them.

It was Kiisa himself that first found what he thought were reliable signs of their trail. He blew his horn. He paused to hear the other hunters blow their horns in response. Nothing! He blew harder, but there was no response. He wondered where the others were and how they could have travelled so far in a short time. He put his hunting bag down and bent down to further examine the trail which he had found. He walked slowly away from his bag as he probed the surrounding bush with a stick. He did not see it coming. He felt a punch-like liquid jet hit his eyes and face. His hands shot to his face to rub off the liquid. The liquid, jelly-like dried up quickly like wax in his hands. He tried to open his eyes. They were gummed shut. Kiisa realized that a snake had spat into his eyes. He was blinded. He had the antidote in his bag. He needed to get to his bag very fast. He tried to navigate his way back to where he had left his bag. The pains in his eyes disoriented him. He scrambled further into the bush in the opposite direction to where he had left his bag. He stumbled and fell flat on his face. He howled in agony, but no one could hear him. Exhausted, he lost consciousness.

He was found dead two days later.

All the other hunters also had misfortunes and none of them returned to the village alive. A tree fell on one, another stepped into a snare set by another hunter for animals, one was attacked and gored by an antelope; and the others simply disappeared and were never heard of again.

For the second time, which coincided with the seventh day the child was born in the nearby bush, The Regulators again filed into Yiofikun's compound. This was an exceedingly rare event that had never happened before in the history of the people of the village. The people had assembled in the compound prior to their arrival. Many were in the mourning clothes and were angry because of the death and disappearance of the hunters. People spoke in low voices.

Everyone fell silent when The Regulators arrived. This time, they were all holding long iron rods decked with cowrie rattles. They stood in a semicircle in the middle of the compound. Their *Atokun*, holding a horn filled with a piece of red cloth soaked in palm stood at a distance in front of the semicircle attentive to the declaration of The Regulators.

The Regulators spoke in low tones and their leader informed the *Atokun* of their decision. The *Atokun* announced, "The child born here in this compound seven days ago is guilty of the murder of our famous hunters. The *abami* boy, born in this compound seven days ago is hereby condemned to the most horrendous death. This sentence is valid for as long as he lives, if he ever steps on the soil of this village. If perchance he is not found and executed before he dies, his first son shall carry the sentence. So shall it be!" As the *Atokun* concluded, The Regulators struck their long iron rods on the ground. The rattles frightened the villagers. They had never seen anything like this before. The Regulators filed out of the compound and the crowd dispersed.

XVI

Back in Betu-Ifẹ, on the seventh day after the arrival of the family in Yonda's house, the boy was named and circumcised according to Yiofikun's people tradition. Coincidentally, this was also the practice in Betu-Ifẹ. Yonda's father invited the Oluawo of the village to conduct the solemn ceremony. Many village elders were also present. It was a day of joy and celebration. Goats that would later be slaughtered and cooked were tied to tree stumps in the compound.

The Oluawo and the elders arrived very early in the morning to conduct the ceremony. It was duty of the Oluawo to circumcise the boy. The Oluawo was an old wiry man with very sharp eyes that gave the impression that he could see beyond the physical world. He muttered incantations as he arrived in the compound. He could not remember how many boys he had circumcised in the village and surrounding villages.

He went into the house. Murewa was seated beside Yiofikun on the floor with the baby in her arms. Abike and Rojoyin were seated behind her. The elders sat also on the floor in a semicircle, their legs folded under them. Oluawo moved to the center of the semicircle and sat on the floor. He brought out a piece of white cloth, spread it on the floor and put the sixteen sacred Ifa palm-nuts (*ikin*) on the cloth.

The child would be named first and circumcised afterwards. For the naming ceremony, the parents of the child had prepared the necessary items in small clay bowls for the ceremony. There was salt, honey, kola-nuts, bitter-kola, alligator pepper, water and *aadun* (beancake). Oluawo gave a cowry to Yiofikun and told him to whisper the name that he wanted the child to be known by on the cowry and return it to him. Yiofikun took the cowry and whispered the name that he had agreed with his household to call the little boy on the cowry. He returned it to Oluawo, who put it on the piece of white cloth. The Oluawo gathered the *ikin* and threw them on the white cloth. It was time to ask Olodumare the name to call the boy. He shuffled the *ikin* left and right and frowned. He looked up at Yiofikun and said, "The name you have chosen is not acceptable! Orunmila, the voice of Olodumare has another name for the boy!"

The elders were baffled. This was the first time they had witnessed a situation like this. They all turned their gaze on Yiofikun, who was confused. He muttered to himself. Seeing his discomfiture, Oluawo asked him what name he had wanted to give the child. He said, "O'Fikun." He then added, "I accept any name that Ifa says."

Oluawo took the ikin again and threw them on the cloth. He again shuffled them left and right, nodded and said, "The same name has come up again." Then he cleared his throat and said, "The name given to this boy from heaven is YESU and by the power of Olodumare, this is what he will be called and how he shall be known!"

It was a strange name. It did not exist in any of the clans that the elders knew. Yiofikun had never heard the name either. It was a special name. Yiofikun nodded his assent. Murewa smiled. Abike and Rojoyin patted her on the back and hugged her. The elders also nodded their assent.

Oluawo asked to carry the boy in his arms. It was time to move to the next stage. The man dipped his little finger in water and rubbed it on the lips of the baby and said, "This is water. Water has no enemies. You will overcome all your enemies. It is the giver of life. Your life will be peaceful like a banana tree planted by a river. You will never be thirsty for good things."

Then, he took a pinch of salt, rubbed it on the baby's lips and said, "This is salt. Nothing preserved in salt ever spoils. It is used to season food to make it palatable. Your life will not know any bitterness. Your life will bring blessings to many."

Oluawo then dipped his little finger in the pot of honey and rubbed it on the baby's lips, saying, "This is honey. It is sweet. Your life will be sweet like honey. You will not know any sorrows."

Then, he pinche a bit of *aadun* and rubbed it on the baby's lips saying, "this is *aadun*. It is a product of human endeavor that nourishes the body. All products of human endeavor shall agree with you and nourish your body. They will not harm you."

Oluawo took the alligator pepper, broke it and said, "this is *atare* (alligator pepper). It has many seeds. Your children will be as many or more than the seeds in this *atare*."

He took the kola-nut, broke it into pieces, held a piece to the child's mouth and said, "This is kola-nut. *Obi! Obi ni nbi ibi danu*! May no harm ever come your way! No evil shall overcome you!"

Finally, he took the bitter-kola, broke it, rubbed a piece on the child's lip and said, "This is *orogbo*! Wa gbo! Wa to! You will live long."

It was time to circumcise the boy. He took out a sharp stone from his bag. It was the same stone that he had used for many circumcisions. His father, from whom he had inherited the stone had used the same implement to circumcise many boys too. Hs father had inherited the same stone from his own father.

Everyone waited for the moment. Tradition demanded that at the first cut, when the baby cried out, the goats tethered for the ceremony in the compound would be slaughtered. The kola-nuts and the bitter kola would be shared out among the elders present.

Oluawo circumcised the boy with the ancient stone. As he cried out, the goats tethered in the compound for celebration feast were slaughtered.

XVII

Yiofikun built his own house in Betu-Ifẹ and his family moved there. Yonda was a constant visitor in their house. She loved Yesu as much as the other women in the household. She would carry him the whole day on her back and only gave the boy to his mother to feed. Murewa, Abike and Rojoyin took turns to carry the baby on their backs too.

When Yesu was about nine months, Abike and Rojoyin became pregnant after several years. It was a joyous moment in the household, and everyone anticipated the arrival of the children. Yonda, clad in white, visited one day with her parents. Yiofikun and his household were happy to receive them. After they had all eaten, Yonda's father explained to Yiofikun that they had come to visit for a purpose. He nodded to Yonda. Yonda, embarrassed cleared her throat and said, "Thank you my father. You all know that I am now at the age to be married. I have many suitors and there had been one young man that I thought I would like to marry. But things have changed!" Abike exchanged glances with Rojoyin and Murewa and they smiled. They thought they were going to get a fourth wife in the household. They were very pleased. They all loved Yonda. Everyone was attentive as Yonda continued, "I have decided on advice and with the consent of my parents not to marry anyone!" Yiofikun and his wives were shocked. It was Murewa who spoke first. "Why? What happened?"

"It is a long story, but I will narrate it! I went to the river a few days ago and on my way back, I saw a man in white billowing robes with a staff in his hand coming from the opposite direction. As he approached me, I saw that the face looked old in one moment and young at the other moment. His dark eyes were very intense. I could not look into his eyes. I greeted him and he answered me in a very strange voice and accent. Then he said, "you are blessed my daughter, the dedicated servant of the Son of Olodumare! The Son is already among you! You must always be clad in white.""

Murewa and Yiofikun immediately understood what had happened. "And what happened afterwards?" Abike asked. Yonda continued, "I was terrified. I wanted to ask him questions, but I could not open my mouth until he left. I ran home to tell my parents the story and we went to Oluawo to find out."

"And what did Oluawo say?" Yiofikun asked. His heart was beating fast. Yonda said, "that is the curious thing. He said, "Yonda! You are blessed my daughter, the dedicated servant of the Son of Olodumare! The Son is already among us! You must always be clad in white." My father wanted to know more. Oluawo after many divinations said he suspected that the child in reference is Yesu! That is why I am wearing white as directed. My parents have agreed that I follow the instructions. It is my destiny and I accept it gladly." She got up from where she was seated and went towards Murewa who was carrying the baby. She knelt beside her and said, "the mother of my Lord" then she bowed before the little boy, who had been curiously looking at everyone, and said, "My Lord, your maidservant is here. I will serve you with my life all my life." She took the boy from Murewa's hand and sat beside her.

Yonda's father got up from his seat, walked slowly to Murewa. He knelt before the boy, and said,

"Olúwa Olódùmarè, Oluaye!
Nígbà yìi ni ó tó jòwó ọmọ ọdò rẹ lówó lọ,

ní Àláàfíà, gẹ́gẹ́ bí ọ̀rọ̀ rẹ:
Nítorí tí ojú mi ti rí ìgbàlà rẹ ná,
Tí ìwọ ti pèsè sílẹ̀ níwájú ènìyàn gbogbo."

He got up and came back to his seat.

Yiofikun turned to him and could see that the old man had tears in his eyes. There was an awkward silence. Then, Yiofikun asked the old man what next steps they needed to take. The man looked up slowly and said, "Mine is to depart in peace to my maker! Yonda has expressed herself. She will stay here with the child. Everyone has his or her own role as concerns the child. It is a matter of destiny. *Ayanmọ̀*!" He got up from his seat, beckoned to his wife and they both left quietly.

Abike, Rojoyin and Murewa welcomed Yonda into their household. Her things were moved into Murewa's room.

XVIII

Yesu grew up like any other child. He was showered with a lot of affection by the four women. Yiofikun had a relationship of respect towards him. From the age of eight years, he started following his father out to fix roofs, construct windows and doors and build houses. Yonda never left him out of her sight. She followed him on all his outings even when he went out with his father to work. She would find a quiet shade and sit down watching the boy.

It was Yonda that took Yesu to Oluawo to learn Ifa. Oluawo was reluctant at the beginning, saying it was he that needed to learn from the boy. But with Yonda's persuasion, he agreed to take on the boy as an Ifa apprentice. Oluawo introduced him to the fundaments of Ifa Corpus. He first learnt the names of the two hundred and fifty-six books or *odus* and *omo-odus*. He learnt the verses of each *odu* by heart and within one year, he could recite any of the four hundred and thirty thousand and eighty verses of the Ifa Corpus. Oluawo knew this was divine knowledge as it took about twenty-one or more years to know a fraction of the verses. No Babalawo knew all the verses. They had areas of speciality, which meant that a Babalawo could be well versed in the some *odus* and *omo-odus*, its verses and interpretations as well as sacrifices, while another in another place would master other *odus* and *omo-odus*. This spread of knowledge informed the necessity that a Babalawo needed to travel from one place to the other to seek out other Babalawos with areas of speciality other than his to learn more and exchange knowledge. Each period of apprenticeship could last as long as seven years. But the young Yesu mastered the entire Ifa Corpus in one year.

Once every five years, Babalawos from different parts of the country had a meeting, where they shared knowledge. It was called Ifa Confraternity Meeting. It was a very big event that lasted about five days. It was only the old Babalawos, who had more than fourteen years of post-initiation stage that participated in the meeting. While each Babalawo was allowed to bring one person at the initiation stage along, these new initiates were not allowed to participate at the meeting. Their role was to attend to the needs of the senior Babalawos.

Oluawo took Yesu to the meeting that held that year. They left three days before the meeting was to hold. Yonda accompanied them. They travelled during the day and rested at night in the villages along the way. People happily received them into their homes, gave them food and the men sat with them in the evenings to get news of other communities. Yonda spoke very little during these stops and kept a vigilant eye on Yesu.

They had to cross a lake, Lake Adagun to reach the village of the meeting. While they waited at the banks of the lake for a canoe to take them across, a canoe with fishermen arrived very close to where they were standing. The fishermen were angry, and some of them were drunk. They had spent many hours on the lake trying to catch fish, but they caught nothing. It was their unlucky day. Their nets were empty.

Oluawo negotiated with them to take them to the other side of the river. Not wanting to go home empty handed, the captain of the fishermen agreed to the number of the cowries that Oluawo offered to ferry them to the other side. It was the first time that Yesu would board a canoe since he was brought as a new-born.

They boarded the canoe. Yesu was excited to be on the canoe. He looked closely at the captain as he steered the canoe. When the canoe was about mid-lake, he told the captain to tell his men to throw their net to the right side of the canoe. The captain was furious. "What are you talking about boy? What do you know about fishing? You just said this is your first time on a canoe. Keep quiet my boy!" Yesu looked calmly at him and said, "what do you lose if you do not catch anything? You said you have been at it since last night! Try!"

The captain of the canoe ordered his men to cast the nets to the right side of the canoe as Yesu had advised. The men threw the nets. Suddenly, their canoe lost its balance. It skewed to the right. The fishermen shouted, "the net has hooked something at the bottom of the lake." Afraid that the canoe might capsize, some of them rushed to the oars and paddled the canoe towards the opposite shore. They pulled the nets along despite the enormous drag on the canoe. Yesu was excited. He told the captain, "I told you!" The captain, afraid of losing his canoe and his men told him angrily, "Shut up, Boy! That's not fish! The net has hooked something at the bottom of the river!"

When they finally arrived at the shore, and the fishermen dragged out the net, they were surprised at the quantity and the size of fish that they had caught. They all looked curiously at Yesu. They removed their caps to salute him. The captain, seeing his luck told Yesu, "My boy, don't ever cross this lake with anyone's canoe except mine. And it is for free. I will take you anywhere you want to go!" Yesu smiled.

Oluawo and Yesu, with Yonda in tow, left the shore and took the bush-path that would take them to the village of the meeting.

Finally, they arrived in the late afternoon at the village where the meeting was holding. For unknown reasons, the inhabitants of this village gave them a very special welcome. Goats and roosters were slaughtered, and food prepared. Every household wanted them to visit. Yesu was very happy with this arrangement. He and Oluawo as well as Yonda visited almost every household in the village and ate to their satisfaction. They slept over in one of the houses.

The meeting began the next day after their arrival. It held under a very big tree. Mats had been spread under the huge shade of the tree. The old Babalawos greeted each other as they arrived and took their seats on the mat. The new initiates who accompanied the Babalawos sat together at a distance from the old men.

Oluawo and Yesu with Yonda were the last to arrive. Oluawo signalled to Yonda to take her seat with the new initiates. The men were surprised. Women were not allowed in their gathering. They looked curiously and did not answer when Yonda greeted them. They moved away from her as she took her seat regally on the mat. The men exchanged glances but did not say anything to Yonda. Yonda ignored them and kept her eyes fastened on Yesu as he accompanied Oluawo to the assembly of the old Babalawos.

The old Babalawos who sat in a circle were shocked when young Yesu took his seat beside Oluawo. They looked at the boy, looked at Oluawo and exchanged glances between themselves. The oldest of them greeted Oluawo and asked him why he brought a pre-initiate to their meeting. Oluawo cleared his throat and said the boy is the most knowledgeable Babalawo he has met in his forty-five years of practice. When the other Babalawos realized that Oluawo was not joking, they were scandalized and felt insulted that Oluawo would rank a prepubescent above them all.

The old man turned to Oluawo and said, "Oluawo, you are a very respectable Babalawo with many years of experience. And many apprentices who have passed by your place respect your profound knowledge of Ifa. You are not known for frivolous remarks, but from what you said, I believe that you are even rating this young boy's knowledge above our own. How can this be? Is there any problem?"

Oluawo looked round at the assembly and said, "Agba-Awo, my dear friend and highly respected colleague, our people say that the spoken word is like a raw egg, the moment a word is uttered, it is like breaking an egg on a rock. It splatters its contents either as truth or as a lie. Whichever it is, the egg cannot be reassembled. My word is my bond. The young man here has unmatched and yet to be seen knowledge of Ifa."

Agba-Awo consulted with the others and said, "We believe you. But as our people say, "*Oju awo ni awo fi ngba obe*. The bowl does not shy away from the hot sauce. With your permission we will put the boy to test." Oluawo nodded his assent.

One by one, the Babalawos put tough question to him. They asked him to recite verses of different *odus* and *omo-odus*. They asked for interpretations of the verses and the appropriate sacrifices. He answered all their questions very calmly. The new initiates seeing what was happening at a distance moved closer to hear the boy answer the questions. Yonda also came.

Yesu explained the Ifa Corpus to the extent that none of the Babalawos had ever heard. This went on till sunset when Agba-Awo told him to stop. They were all amazed. None of them had ever seen something like this. Politely, Yesu asked them if he could ask all of them a question on Ifa. They hesitantly agreed. His knowledge had dazzled them. Oluawo nudged him and told him it was not necessary. Oluawo knew that none of them would be able to answer and he wanted to save them from embarrassment.

Agba-Awo looked at Yesu and asked the question that was on the mind of all the Babalawos, "my boy, how could you have mastered the entire Ifa corpus in one year? Tell us, please!"
Yesu shrugged and said, "my father taught me."
"Your father? You mean Oluawo?" about three or four Babalawos asked simultaneously.
Yesu shook his head.

One of the Babalawos asked Oluawo if the boy's father was also a Babalawo. Oluawo shook his head to answer.

"Which father then?" the assembly was curious to know the source. Many were thinking of also going to the source to increase their knowledge.

The boy shrugged and said, "My father!" He got up from the mat and sought out Yonda, who already had a calabash of cool water for him.

One Babalawo, seeing the interaction between Yonda and Yesu asked Oluawo, "is that his mother? Why is she clad in white?" Oluawo answered, "no. that is not his mother. She is a servant dedicated to the boy!"

This added to the mystery. Many of them brought out their *opele*, (divination chain) to consult Ifa on who exactly the boy was. "What did you say his name was again?" one asked.

"Yesu!" replied Oluawo.

There was silence as the Babalawos did their consultation with Ifa. When done with their consultations, they packed their *opele* in their bags and stood up and walked in a single file to where Yesu and Yonda sat. One by one, they knelt before the boy, bowed their heads to the floor and said, "Master!" Yesu acknowledged their greetings very calmly.

By the time the last Babalawo left the meeting place, the whole village had heard about the events of the day. Many villagers came to the meeting place to invite Yesu to come to their house for dinner and pass the night. Yesu fastened his eyes on a destitute woman, a widow of many years and told her, "we will have dinner with you and stay the night in your place." The woman was alarmed. She had only come to see the boy and not to invite him. She did not have any food in her poor home. The woman said, "Master, I have no food. I have no money and my shelter in very poor." Yesu simply replied, "my father will provide. Let us go to your house."

The news immediately spread in the village that young Yesu and his entourage was going to pass the night in the poor widow's house. By the time Yesu and his entourage got the house, many villagers had already arrived with many gifts for Yesu. Some brought cooked food, some brought raw food, some brought goats and sheep, some brought clothes, and many brought money. Yesu gladly received all the gifts from them. He, Oluawo, Yonda and the poor widow sat with the visitors and ate to their satisfaction. There was a lot of left-over food which the widow diligently packed and stored. Early the next morning, Yesu gave all the money and other gifts to the widow.

They left the house and made their way to the meeting place. It was the second day of the meeting. As Yesu and Oluawo with Yonda in tow arrived at the meeting place, all the Babalawos stood up and bowed to Yesu. They waited until he sat down on the mat before they took their seats. The day went fast. It was to Yesu that the old Babalawos directed their questions on different *odus* and *omo-odus* and the necessary procedures and sacrifices to address different issues. Yesu patiently answered their questions and explained many other things to them. The day went by very fast and when the meeting ended, Yesu and his entourage of Oluawo and Yonda spent the night in another villager's house.

The Babalawos didn't disperse immediately after the meeting. They stayed back after Yesu and his entourage had left to discuss on the two days of the meeting.

"This is a wonder. A boy of nine years with the knowledge of the ancients!"

"Yes! He is the Son of the Ancient One, no doubt!"

"I had thought he was the third reincarnation of Orunmila. But we all know that Orunmila, after his second reincarnation refused to come to the earth again after his rift with Ọlọwọ̀. We all remember how Ejiogbe, Orunmila's most senior apostle reported the exchange between Orunmila and his sons. So, Yesu is certainly not Orunmila's reincarnate. He is a class on his own."

"I am thinking of inviting him to my domain for some years to learn from him" Agba-Awo suddenly interjected.

"I was thinking of the same thing too!"

"Me too!" soon rented the air.

Agba-Awo exhorted them to work out a calendar of stay of Yesu in their different domains. There were ten of them including Agba-Awo and Oluawo. They all agreed that they would propose to Oluawo that Yesu spent two years with each of them. Agba-Awo wanted him for three years. This arrangement meant Yesu would spend twenty-one years of his life teaching the Babalawos. He would be thirty when done.

At the meeting the next day, the plan was revealed to Yesu and Oluawo. Oluawo deferred to Yesu to make his decision. Yesu beckoned to Yonda and told her of the plan. "Whatever my Master decides," she said. Yesu turned to the assembly and gave his assent. His first sojourn of three years would be with Agba-Awo, he told them. The Babalawos were all very happy. For the first time in known memory, the meeting broke up two days before the normal five days. Oluawo left for Betu-Ifẹ village alone with the promise that he would inform Yesu's parents of the developments. It would take another nineteen years before his parents set eyes on him.

XIX

Yesu spent the following years traveling from one Babalawo to the other teaching them. His adult body gradually emerged from his slender teenage frame. He was very dark-skinned with glittering white teeth and very handsome. He was of medium height and slender. He cut his hair very short and because he despised facial hair, he was always clean shaven. He was very jovial and loved to tell jokes. He loved people around him, and he attended all events like naming ceremony, weddings, and traditional festivals with glee.

Young ladies doted over him hoping to catch his attention for a potential marriage proposal. He loved the attention and he sometimes teased them.

Yonda did not age for all the years she was travelling. She looked the same; always clad in brilliant white. A white woven scarf adored her head. Many men in different villages also took interest in her, but she ignored them all. She was not particularly talkative and did not make many friends during their journey. She was Yesu's mother, sister and friend. On many occasions, Yesu called her his bosom friend. On others, he called her his sister or his mother. Yonda's heart always swelled with joy with these endearments, although she considered herself a simple servant to her Master.

Yesu did not have any possessions. Before he left a village, he gave away all the belongings acquired during his stay. He always arrived in the next village with nothing.

After completing his first three years of teaching Agba-Awo, one of the newly initiated Babalawos under Agba-Awo told the old man that he had decided to follow Yesu on his teaching mission. The old man granted his wish, and when they presented the request to Yesu, he simply smiled, patted the man on the back and said, "you are welcome. It is going to be fun. But see, I do not have any possessions, not a house and no money." The initiate was overjoyed to follow him and to be able to learn directly from him.

After a stay in each of the villages where Yesu had gone to teach the different Babalawos, one initiate would offer to join the group.

Oluawo, in Betu-Ife was the last Babalawo that Yesu had promised to teach the hidden secrets of Ifa Corpus. He was twenty-eight years old when he began the return journey to Betu-Ife where Oluawo and his parents resided. By this time, in addition to Yonda, there were nine Ifa initiates who had abandoned their villages and families to follow him.

Yesu was excited to be going back to Betu-Ife. He had missed his parents all these years. He always thought he had three mothers. He had missed his mothers and was looking forward to seeing them again. He often wondered how many siblings his parents would have endowed him with. He looked forward to meeting them all.

He and his entourage soon arrived at the shores of Lake Adagun. It was the last stretch of their long journey to Betu-Ife. They waited at the shores and soon the canoe of the fishermen that had taken him, Oluawo and Yonda across the lake many years ago arrived. It was the same captain, the same fishermen, now advanced in years. Many of them had grey hairs, some were completely bald. Their wrinkled skins were very dark from the sun. The Captain was bald and had lost most of his teeth. He looked smaller than the last time Yesu saw him. He squinted at Yesu and thought he had seen him before.

"Sir, have we met before?" He asked Yesu.

Yesu smiled, "Yes! Many years ago!"

"Where was that? My memory is playing games with me!"

"Here on the lake. You caught a lot of fish on that day when I came here in your canoe!"

"The Boy? My Boy?"

Yesu nodded and smiled.

The old Captain gave him his whole toothless smile and hugged him. "I remember my promise my boy! Get on the canoe. You have grown into a fine young man! So happy to see you. We want more fish this time!"

Yesu boarded the canoe, and his entourage followed suit.

"Who are these people?" the captain demanded.

"My people!" Yesu answered.

"But how are we going to fish with this multitude in my canoe?"

"Forget about the fish. The people are more important. Fishing people is more important!"

"What does that mean? Fishing people? What are you talking about my Boy?"

"You will understand someday! Let us go!"

"Ok, but I am not happy. My promise was based on the premise that you would come alone on my canoe and indicate the location of fish in the lake for me. Now you are talking about fishing people. Whoever heard of fishing people out of a lake?"

Yesu smiled and again said, "You will understand someday!"

The captain expertly turned the canoe and began to steer it to the other shore.

"What is your name by the way my Boy?"

"Yesu! And you are Omiroke or Miroke, the son of Omimuyi, the son of Omifohun!"

"How could you know that? Who told you? Even my men do not know my real name. Everyone knows me as Iwin Adagun!"

"I just know it. I even know the names of your wives and children too!"

"I don't believe you! OK! Tell me the name of my latest wife!"

"Orogbomi from Betu-Apata!"

"What? How can you possibly know that? I just married her!"

"I know many things."

Just as the Captain was going to make a remark, a huge wave hauled up the canoe, jarred it violently in its crest and then slammed it into its trough. The passengers screamed. It was evident that with a few more waves like that, the canoe would capsize. A bigger wave started building at a distance and coming fast towards the canoe. The Captain looked wildly at his passengers and saw that Yesu was calm and was smiling!

"Do something, my Boy! Save us!" he yelled.

Yesu stood up in the middle of the boat despite the heaving and hauling, looked calmly at the approaching wave, and stretched out his hand with his open palm facing the oncoming wave. To the amazement of all the passengers, the wave fizzled out. The lake became very calm.

The Captain spat into the water. He was angry. He turned to Yesu, "Did you bring that wave? Did you cause the wave? I had never seen anything

like that in my twenty-five years on this lake!
What are you trying to prove?"
Yesu smiled but did not reply.
"I am withdrawing my promise. I won's carry you
on this canoe again. You can board any canoe you
want, but not this!"
Yesu smiled and did not say anything,
They soon reached the shore and the passengers
disembarked, Yesu thanked the Captain and said,
"see you soon, Fisher of Men!"
The Captain spat into the water. He did not reply.

Yesu and his entourage were hungry and tired.
They had been travelling since the evening of the
previous day and their experience on the lake had
exhausted them all. They had their last meal more
than half a day ago. They needed food and rest
before continuing their journey. Yesu found a
slopy grove and invited his entourage to rest there.

The only food they had was a baked yam, which
the wife of the last initiate to join the group had
put in his bag. Yesu sat down on a tree stump to
think. After a moment, he sent Yonda to Iwin
Adagun, the Captain of the canoe that brought
them earlier. "Tell him to give us some fish," he
told Yonda. He asked two of the initiates to get
some firewood and start a fire in which they

would roast the fish. The initiates remembered the animosity of the Captain towards Yesu and wondered if the man would give them any fish. They however did as Yesu said and soon the fire was burning while everyone waited for Yonda.

Yonda soon arrived with five small fish strung on a small rope. She told them that that was all the Captain had. They roasted the fish on the fire. Yesu, Yonda and nine initiates sat down to share five fish and one baked yam. As they ate, they heard voices approaching them. The Captain, who had felt remorse at the way he treated Yesu on his canoe led ten of his men to the grove to see Yesu and if possible, to apologize to him. Yesu was happy to see them and invited them to join them at the feast. The fishermen sat down and ate with them. Some passengers who wanted to cross the lake, who had been looking for the Captain and had found him at the feast also joined them. When they had all eaten their maximum feel, they packed the remnants that could still feed many people. Some of the initiates wanted to stuff their bags with some of the remnants. Yesu shook his head.

The Captain called Yonda aside and asked her, "where did you get more fish? I gave you only five."

"It was the five fish we have been eating!"

"You mean no one gave you more fish?"

"Uhm…uhm."

"And the yam? Where did it come from?"

"One of my colleagues had a baked yam. That is what we all shared."

"You mean all of us ate five fish and one yam?"

"Yes!" Yonda smiled.

The Captain rubbed his eyes, shook his head, and asked, "Who is this man?"

"Yesu!"

"Where is he from? Do you know his parents?"

"From Betu-Ife. Yes. I know his parents very well."

The Captain was lost in thoughts for some moments. Yonda looked at him. Then he said, "I don't want to captain the canoe anymore. I don't need to work anymore. I am also going to follow him. My heart tells me that he will provide all my needs and the needs of my family."

Yonda smiled and said, "let us go and tell him."

They found Yesu chatting with the initiates, the fishermen and the passengers. He was telling them something that made all of them laugh. He was in a very good mood. He looked up as Yonda and the Captain approached and said, "Miroke, the heart does not deceive. You have done well by listening to your heart! You are welcome."

The Captain was dazed. How could he have known what he discussed with Yonda? While he was still wondering, Yesu said, "as I tell everyone, you can see that I do not have any possessions, no house, and no money. But you are welcome. It is going to be fun."

"Thank you, my B…uh, thank you Master."

One of the Captain's crew asked him what he wanted them to do with the canoe. "It is all yours, but we won't pay whenever the Master needs it." Everyone laughed.

Miroke, the Captain asked Yesu for permission to run a quick errand for someone. Yesu smiled and said, "Miroke, the face tells the truth even when the mouth denies it. Go quickly!"

Miroke's jaw dropped. "This man reads peoples' minds," he thought as he sadly left the group to go on his errand. His heart was heavy. He realized that he had been caught in a lie. He walked slowly along the bush-path to his destination. A thought suddenly occurred to him and he shouted, "I will never tell lies again. I will be straight as an oar!" This thought relieved him. His heart became lighter and realizing that Yesu and his entourage could leave before he got back, he ran very fast to his destination. It was to his brother's place that he went.

Aken, Miroke's brother was a drummer. Although he came from a family of fishermen on Lake Adagun's shores, he hated the lake and fishing. His life was playing his drum in his small village ensemble which an old musician had put together to entertain guests at festivals and important events. Sometimes, in-between parties, Aken played as an itinerant drummer moving from one small village to the other to raise money for himself. Unmarried, Aken was poor but happy. His joy was in making people happy with his drum.

Miroke arrived in his brother's compound panting. He was happy to find his brother at home. He had been apprehensive that Aken would have gone out drumming. Miroke doing away with greetings and niceties urgently implored his brother, "get you drum Aken. Let us go now!" Aken, having never seen his laid-back brother like this, ran into his hut, emerged with his drum and ran after his brother. They paused to catch their breath after a few moments. Breathlessly, Aken asked his brother what the problem was.

"I have found solution to our problems."

"What solution?"

"I met a man who knows what everyone is thinking. He stopped a vicious wave on the lake with his mere hand. He fed many people with just one yam and five fish."

"Are you serious?"

"Oh yes! We don't ever have to work again to eat. We can even ask him to conjure as much money as we want. I have left the Lake to follow him, and you are coming with me. No more itinerant drumming and begging."

"You have left the Lake? And your canoe?

"I gave it away! Why work if I can get free food?"

"You gave away your canoe? It is very serious then. I am convinced! Let us go my brother. But…?"

"But what?"

"My drum! My life as a musician! Do you think he will accept me?"

"Of course! He is very easy going. He laughs a lot and likes to tell jokes. He doesn't judge anybody. You just need to trust him. And no lies, Aken! He will know it even before you utter it."

"And my drum and music?"

"I am sure he will love it. Let us quickly go and meet him!"

Yesu was happy to see Aken!

"Aken, my man!"

Aken knelt and bowed, and said, "I am all yours Master! But how did you know my name?"

"It doesn't matter. My father and I know many things even before they come to be!"

"Thank you, Master! I brought my drum too!" he showed his drum to Yesu.

"Oh yes. Eat first. There is yam and fish. Maybe you can entertain us after you have eaten!"

"Oh yes! Oh yes! Thank you Master!"

Miroke found food for his brother.

Yesu cracked jokes as everyone waited for Aken to finish his meal. They wanted to hear him play and they all, even the normally quiet Yonda, looked forward to dancing to his music.

Aken announced his readiness by sounding some notes on his drum as he moved towards where Yesu sat. Yesu got up, started singing a lively song and they all joined in, with Aken's drum accompaniment. Soon everyone started clapping and dancing to the music. Aken drummed his best on this day.

They sang and danced until almost sunset. Yesu decided that they would all camp there for the night. The next morning, Yesu and his followers now twelve, comprising of Yonda, Miroke and his brother, Aken and nine Ifa initiates departed the shores of Lake Adagun and set out for Betu-Ife. Yesu had decided that their first port of call would be his parents' house.

XX

Back in Betu-Ife, Yiofikun had aged considerably. He suffered from arthritis in his joints and his sight had dimmed considerably. Most of his teeth had fallen off. His back was bent, and he walked with a staff. Although years had left some lines on their faces, Abike, Rojoyin and Murewa still looked considerably younger than their ages.

Their compound was much larger. Yiofikun had expanded the compound many years ago to accommodate his large family. While Yesu was away, Abike had four children, (two boys and two girls), Rojoyin had five (four boys and one girl) and Murewa had six (three boys and three girls). All the girls had married and left, while all the males had built their own houses within the compound and they had all married too. Yiofikun had twelve grandchildren by the time Yesu returned home. He was called *Baba Agba*, the Patriarch. His compound was called Keur Ibukun.

It was Abike that answered when some visitors announced their presence in their compound by clapping. The others were having a siesta. She squinted in the harsh sun to identify any of the visitors. She recognized Yonda among them. Yonda had not changed. She opened her mouth and ran back into the house. She hurried woke everyone up and said, "I think Yesu is back!" The three women scrambled out of the house leaving Yiofikun to find his own way out. It was Murewa that first recognized her son among the visitors. She threw her hands out to hug him, but Abike blocked her. "It may be his ghost!" Abike shouted. The women scramble around the compound for sand, which they scooped with their hands and threw on Yesu. It was believed that whenever people died in a foreign land after a long sojourn, their ghosts would appear in their place of birth. In order to ensure that the apparition did not permanently escape into the spirit world, sand had to be poured on such a relative that just appeared after not being seen for many years. The person should not be touched before this ritual, otherwise the person would disappear never to be seen again. Yesu laughed as his mothers bathed him with sand. Satisfied that Yesu was not apparition and reassured that even he was, he would not escape into the spirit world again, the three women threw themselves upon him. They cried as they hugged him. They asked him many questions as they examined him from head to toe.

Rojoyin went into the house to get mats to spread under the shade of the tree for Yesu and his entourage. Murewa went to get them water and Abike went to get Yesu's siblings who were in their homes in the compound.

Yesu's siblings rushed out of their houses to meet their brother. They had heard many stories about him from their mothers. Yesu stood up as they approached him and hugged them one by one. They told him their names. None of them looked like Yesu. They all looked like Yiofikun with little admixture from their mothers. Yesu was excited to meet his brothers. He asked after their work and after their families.

As Yesu and his siblings were discussing, Yiofikun made his way slowly out of the house towards them, Yesu and his nine siblings got up from the mat to meet him. They all prostrated before him to greet him. He told them to stand up and he looked in the direction of Yesu. He took some steps towards him and hugged him, muttering, "Welcome back, Son of the Most High!" Yesu smiled and bowed again before Yiofikun. The old man pulled him to himself and whispered, "I am happy the way I am. It is the way Olodumare wants me to be in my old age. Do not do anything to change my present condition." Yesu cried as he nodded. He gently guided the old man to the mat to sit down.

The women were up and about setting up to prepare a feast. Yonda also joined them. She learnt from the women that her father and mother had died many years ago and had left their house to one of her cousins. She cried silently when she had the news. Murewa informed her that her mother left her something she said she had also inherited from her own mother, who had also inherited it from her mother. The old woman showed Murewa where she hid the object.

Murewa promised to go with Yonda to her parents' house after the feast.

Yonda wondered what it was that her mother had bequeathed to her. She thought of her childhood and tried to remember all the interactions that she had with her mother and the stories she told her. Then she remembered a story her mother had told her of her great grandfather, Efunlaya. Efunlaya, in his young days was an adventurous person who travelled far and wide in search of knowledge and other cultures. Whenever he came back from any of his journeys, the elders of the village would invite him to tell them the tales of his journeys, which he gladly did. He brought many seeds and fruits back from his journeys to try in his native soil.

His parents prevailed on him to settle down and marry which he deftly dodged. His parents, horrified that he would bring home a foreign wife from one of his journeys decided to find him a local girl. He told them that he would marry her when he returned from his next journey. He left on his trip and nothing was heard from him for many years. His parents and siblings gave him up for dead. The girl that they had intended him to marry went off to marry another man.

He returned home eight years later. He had married a foreigner and had a little baby girl. The parents were very happy to see their son and they gladly accepted the foreign wife who could not speak their language. The foreign wife was Yonda's great grandmother and the little girl they brought home was her grandmother.

Efunlaya narrated the tales of this long trip to the elders of the village as was his habit. He told them of people with pale skin that he had met; he told of people with brown skin, and of people with what he called curious slant of eyes. He told them of the mutual curiosity of meeting with these peoples. He lived and worked in these places. His wife was given to him by one chief in the land of the brown people. There in this land, it was the girl's parents who gave dowry to the husband. Among many other things, Efunlaya was given a small metal container with *champaca* oil which he gave to his wife. Before her great grandmother died, she gave the container to her grandmother, who later passed it to her mother. Yonda suspected that this was what her mother had bequeathed to her.

XX

While Yesu and the others waited for the food to be served, his sisters arrived with their husbands and their children. Yesu was very happy to see them all and to see his little nieces and nephews. He played hide and seek with them and told them stories.

Soon food was served. As they ate, Yesu told them stories and cracked jokes with the others. Yonda reminded Murewa of her promise and both of them quietly sneaked away to go to Yonda's parents' house. Yonda's cousin who lived in the house with his family was very happy to see her. He asked his wife to cook some food for Yonda and Murewa, which they both politely refused. They invited him to join them with his family in Yiofikun's compound. Yonda explained the purpose of their visit.

Murewa pointed to a corner in the room where Yonda's mother had lived and said that was the place where the mother indicated. Yonda's cousin gently dug up the place. He soon discovered a wooden box filled with dry leaves and twigs. He brought it out and gave it to Yonda. There was an earthen pot also filled with leaves in the box. Yonda gently took it out. She removed the leaves and found a smaller earthen pot. She took it out. Inside it, wrapped in a small piece of cloth was a sealed vial. Yonda knew shea had guessed right. She took the vial and put it in the fold of her clothes. She thanked her cousin and she and Murewa left to Yiofikun's compound.

They heard the drumming and the singing in the distance and hurried to go and join the others. Aken was in his elements and everyone was dancing. Two of Yesu's brothers, who also played some musical instruments had also brought out *shekere* and *agogo* to accompany Aken's drum. Yesu, who loved to dance was the most vigorous dancer among the lot. His feet were caked with dust as he stomped them on the soil. His face shone with sweat. Yiofikun, who was a great dancer in his prime, also joined in the dance.

Yiofikun ordered for more palm-wine for everyone. His two sons whom he had sent to get the palm-wine soon returned with a frown on their faces. They had run out of palm-wine. Yiofikun ordered them to go out and buy from the tappers. They came back empty handed. There was no palm-wine. The tappers had sold all their stock for the day. Yiofikun frowned. He did not want the party to end abruptly because there was no palm-wine. Yesu saw Yiofikun discussing with his brothers and went over to know the issue. Yiofikun told him they had run out of palm-wine and his brothers could not get to buy. Yesu told them that there was palm-wine in the big pots at the back of Yiofikun's house. Yiofikun shook his head and said, "No, Son! We only store water in those pots! There is no palm-wine there." Yesu smiled and told one of his brothers to go and get some of the contents from any of the pots. The young man soon returned. Yesu nodded to him to give his father. The old man knew from the colour and the smell that it was high grade palm-wine. He drank it and nodded his pleasure. He looked at Yesu, "Did you put palm-wine in those pots? Did you buy it? When did you buy it?" Yesu smiled and shrugged. Yiofikun ordered his sons to distribute the palm-wine to everyone. As Yesu drank, Yiofikun winked to him and said, "your mothers would be furious with you when they discover that you have filled their waterpots with palm-wine! Just imagine them going to the pots to fetch water to cook or to wash and they discover palm-wine!" They both laughed out loud.

The palm-wine flowed and Aken gave them their best till evening time when they were all exhausted. Some sat on the mats and continued drinking while some lied down. Their feet were dusty with the red earth. Murewa, Abike and Rojoyin sat near Yesu. Yonda got up from where she was seated. She went inside the house and soon emerged with a small pot of water. She took her seat in front of Yesu and washed off the dust from his feet. She then rummaged in the fold of her clothes and brought out the vial which she had inherited from her mother. She broke the seal and poured the contents, the *champaca* oil on Yesu's feet and massaged them.

The fragrant smell of the oil permeated the entire compound and set off small bombs of pleasure in the noses and lungs of the people around. Everyone came nearer to witness Yonda's ritual and to smell the oil at close quarters. No one had ever smelt any fragrance like this before and they all realized that this must be a very expensive oil. Yesu was surprised but was calm as Yonda massaged his feet. Everyone was quiet. It was Miroke that first found his voice and said, "that must be a very expensive oil. I am sure that small vial must cost much more than all the fish in Lake

Adagun! Master must not be allowed to walk on his feet again. We will be carrying him! And he must not wash his feet for the next one year!" Everyone including Yesu laughed. Aken ran off some notes on his drum in praise of Yonda.

The party ended at sunset. As the people departed, they came over to Yesu. They knelt before him to touch his feet. Everyone wanted to carry a bit of the beautiful fragrance with them. Yesu's sisters-in-laws unwrapped their headgears and rubbed their hair in the fragrance on his feet.

When everyone had left, Yiofikun told Yesu that he and his mothers wanted to speak with him alone. Yonda would also participate in the discussion. Yesu told his other eleven followers to move their mats further away. Most of them slept as soon as they moved the mats. They had taken more than enough palm-wine.

Yiofikun cleared his throat and again welcomed Yesu. He prayed for him. He told him of the circumstances of his birth, the events after his birth and how they had to escape with him from Betu-Akara, the land of his birth. He told him that in all probability, The Regulators must have placed an order of capture and death on his head if

he ever set foot on Betu-Akara. Yesu listened calmly through it all, then sighed, "what will be will be as Olodumare has ordained it!" Abike asked him to promise that he would never go there, but Yesu refused very gently. He said he did not want any human agreement to interfere with what Olodumare has set out for him. Murewa told him that it was time to marry and settle down. All his siblings were married and have settled down. Rojoyin said she had identified a fine young girl from a respectable home for him. Yesu smiled and said, "there is no hurry my mothers. Let us be patient. It will happen if Olodumare wishes it."
Yesu told them that he and his followers would be leaving very early the next morning for Oluawo's place and would be resident there for the next two years. The women asked him if they could be visiting him there. Yesu nodded his assent.

Yesu and his followers left very early the next morning for Oluawo's place.
Oluawo, who had been expecting them was very happy to receive Yesu.

Yesu's stay with Oluawo was uneventful.
About a year after he arrived there, one of his brothers came one late afternoon to inform his that Yiofikun was very ill and was probably dying.

Yesu, in the company of Yonda left immediately to go and see Yiofikun. They heard wailing in the distance as they approached the house. Yesu and Yonda ran the remaining short distance to the house.

The women were distraught with grief. Yesu's brothers, though not openly wailing as the women, stood looking with red eyes at the roof. Yesu went into the room where Yiofikun was laid. The women and his brothers had followed him inside. Yesu cried.

He sat beside Yiofikun's body and laid his right hand on his chest. After some moments, Yiofikun opened his eyes, removed Yesu's hand from his chest and held on to the hand as he muttered, "Let your servant depart in peace!" He dropped Yesu's hand.

Yesu wept again. Everyone wept.

Yiofikun was buried in his compound the next day.

XXI

Yesu completed his last year of training of Oluawo uneventfully. He left Oluawo's place and went to stay with his mothers for a short time. One evening, he announced to them that he would be leaving the next day with his followers. The women were worried and asked him the reason for his decision. He told them that he had spent nineteen years of his life teaching the masters of Ifa Corpus and he wanted to take the new message of Ifa and the healing powers Olodumare directly to the common people.

"How?" Murewa asked. She was very worried for her son. She had just lost her husband and was anxious to let her son out of her sight.

"By moving from village to village to share the good news of Olodumare's support to mankind through me."

"But they may not believe you!" Rojoyin interjected.

"Well, that is true. But as many as believe will have a new experience!"

"And what do you expect to get from that, Yesu? It would be tough. Unlike your nine years here with us and the nineteen years you spent teaching the Babalawos when you had food and shelter, going from one village to the other would not provide any of that. Why don't you just settle down here and find a girl to marry, my son?" Abike pleaded.

"See, my mothers! It is not as simple as that. I have been entrusted with a mission and I must carry out the mission irrespective of challenges and difficulties. Please do not make this difficult for me. I will try to be back in three years' time and then we will see about the marriage."

The three women were silent. Yesu asked Yonda to bring some water for him. He washed their feet one by one and they blessed him.

Yesu and his followers set out on their journey early the next day.

XXII

Yesu and his twelve followers did not go in the direction of Lake Adagun, rather they moved in the opposite direction. They travelled throughout the day and did not see any village or human settlement. The feet of the followers were blistered, and they were all tired. There were no big trees under which they could settle for the night. The vegetation was coarse and sparse. And they were all hungry too.

"Master, are we lost?" Miroke asked Yesu.

"I am not sure, but I will know this night!"

"How? I suggest we return to Betu-Ife first thing in the morning!"

"That is out of question Miroke. We must move on."

"I and my colleagues are very hungry and tired. We cannot just be going about in this wild and unfriendly environment that does not have any sign of human habitation!"

"Be patient Miroke!"

Miroke shrugged and went to meet with the others. Yonda sat close to Yesu. Yesu said, "Yonda, everything will be alright. Trust me!"

Yonda nodded and said, "Master, I have never doubted you!"

Darkness soon set in.

Yesu's followers sat in the open field at a distance from Yesu and grumbled. It was a pitch-black night. There was no moon and the stars shone very brightly. Yesu got up from where he was seated and told one of his followers to follow him. They moved a short distance away and Yesu asked the follower if he would be able to find his way to where they were. The man nodded but realizing that Yesu could not see him in the dark, hoarsely responded. Yesu told him to look around him. The man looked around and saw what looked like yams around him and a spring of water just a few paces away. Yesu instructed him to pick one and eat. It was the most delicious baked yam the man had ever eaten in his life. He was dumbfounded. Yesu told him to go and get the others.

Soon the man arrived with the others, and Yesu told them, "Eat and drink!" The followers scrambled for the yams and drank from the spring.

Yesu moved further away and looked into the sky intently. He soon saw the star he was looking for. He waited patiently as his followers ate and drank. When they were done, he asked them if they were still tired.

"I feel as strong as a bull after this meal and I am the oldest in the group!" Miroke responded.

"I am happy to hear that! Olodumare has given us a guide to lead us in our journey! Shall we go on?" They all chorused their assent.

Yesu followed the star as it moved with his followers in tow. By early morning, when the star had disappeared, they were in the vicinity of a big village. They met a woman at a well and Yesu introduced himself and his followers.

"Where are you from?"

"Betu-Ife," he responded.

"What is your name?"

"Yesu!"

"Do you want some water to drink and to wash your feet?"

"Yes! Thank you, Oreke!"

"But I didn't tell you my name. How did you guess?"

"I didn't guess. I just know it. I know about you. You were married to Kegbayi, you left him because you had no children with him, then you married Kedoyin and you left him for the same reason. Now you live with Ketide and you have a daughter called Kekemi!"

The woman, alarmed, fled from the well and ran back to the village. She shouted as she approached the village and people came out of their homes.

They asked her what happened!

She panted, "I just met a stranger at the well who told me everything about my life! He came with some followers who call him Master!"

"Are they armed? History tells us that our forefathers had issues with the people of Betu-Ife." one young man asked.

"I think they have come in peace. They are not armed."

"I suggest we do not take any risks. Let us arm ourselves and accompany Pati to the well. We will deal with them if they have not come in peace."

They found Yesu seated on a rock with his followers around him. They were all relaxed and laughing at a joke that Yesu had told them. The group from Betu-Oke, who had accompanied Oreke to the well greeted Yesu and asked him the purpose of his visit to their village.

"We have come in peace. We are not bearers of hostile history. We are messengers of a peaceful future for mankind. Your village is our first port of call on our peaceful mission."

"You are welcome to Betu-Oke! Please follow us!"

Yesu and his followers spent many months in Betu-Oke. During one of his many conversations with the women in Betu-Oke, he told them that they could have their well closer home instead of going far to fetch water. He told them he had found a place within their village where a well with good water could be dug. The women giggled and shook their heads. They did not want a well close-by. They preferred to travel some distance away from the village to fetch their water. Yesu was curious to know why.

"See! We normally go to the well in small groups. It is the only time we get to freely talk about our husbands and our mothers-in-law. If you sink the well here in the village, then we will lose those precious moments of freedom," Oreke said.

Yesu found this very funny and they all laughed.

During their stay in Betu-Oke, the star that guided them to the village always stayed over the village at night. Yesu decided that they would only embark on their journeys in the night so that they could be guided by the star.

They moved from village to village under the guidance of the star, which Yesu named "Star of Destiny" for a period of three years. In the second year of their travel, the star led them to a small village called Betu-Kari. During their stay there, one of the villagers, Kekoyi, declared himself to have fallen in love with Yonda. Yonda repelled his advances, and this annoyed him greatly. Kekoyi was a member of the seven-man village ruling council, he was rich and had a lot of influence. He had three wives. He repeatedly pestered Yonda and on one occasion, Yonda pushed him off as he tried to touch her. The man fell down and broke his pelvic bones. He could not stand up or move and people had to carry him to his house.

The event became a joke in the village and Kekoyi was the butt of the joke. Known in the village for his philandering, the villagers, particularly the women invented a song to mock him. Even his wives mocked him. Kekoyi felt deeply humiliated. He decided that Yonda was not going to leave their village alive. He called a meeting of the village ruling council in his house to explain what had happened between him and Yonda. He told the members of the council that the force that he felt when Yonda pushed him was like being hit by a huge tree. He said he flew some distance before the force slammed him down hard. He told them that it was dangerous that women should be allowed to have the upper hand in any conflict with any man. He told them to imagine a situation where men were beaten and wounded by their wives. This touched the members of the council and they asked him what he expected them to do about the situation.

"We should beat her to death! She should not be allowed to leave this place alive," Kekoyi said.

"Ahhh….! We can't just do that!" one member said.

"What would we say her offence was? People may rise against us."

"We declare her a witch! Do you not see that she is always dressed in white? Which normal woman wears white every time? She bewitched me!" Kekoyi said.

"Hmm…! But this will be unfair!" a member said.

"Unfair? How can you say that? We must stand together! On whose side do you think I would be if your wife beat you up and broke your bones?"

The man kept quiet. The members of the council were hesitant to follow Kekoyi's idea. Kekoyi understood and had prepared for this. He pulled a big sac to himself and told the men to look inside. It was full of money. "This is all for you! Share it. I have been meaning to give you gifts. This is the right moment." He told one of them to share it out among the others. Greed overwhelmed reason. The men chattered and smiled as heaps of money were placed in front of them. Done with the sharing, Kekoyi cleared his throat and said, "let us go back to the matter at hand."

There was no further dissent to Kekoyi's proposal to kill Yonda. They agreed that the village crier would announce their decision to brand Yonda a witch and to call out the young men to administer the punishment as demanded by tradition.

Yesu was away in the bush to meditate and to get some medicinal leaves when these men conspired against Yonda.

Immediately after the announcement, people came out of their houses. The men were armed with sticks; the women huddled together under a tree.

The men chanted war songs as they marched to the house where Yonda and other Yesu's followers were staying. When Yesu's followers heard the men coming, Miroke told two of the followers to quickly go and look for Yesu and inform him. As the riot noise approached the house, the followers scrambled for safety. Yonda did not move, despite Miroke's insistence that she followed him to safety.

She stepped out of the house and calmly waited for the crowd. They soon seized her. They tied her hands behind her back and dragged her towards the village limits where they intended to beat her with their sticks to death. They soon reached the place of execution. They pushed her down and as they raised their sticks to start hitting her, Yesu appeared with two of his followers in tow. He stood between the executioners and their victim. He looked at each of them in the eyes, and said, "Let he, who was not born of a woman be the first to hit her." He stepped aside, so that the executioners had direct access to their victim. They froze, then one by one, they left. Some threw their sticks away into the bush. Yesu helped Yonda up and said, "I am very sorry this happened Yonda. The heart of man is full of evil. It is our mission to purge their minds of this evil."

Yonda was calm. She brushed off the dust and twigs from her dress.

"Let us go home now. We will leave this village in the evening and move as the Star of Destiny directs," Yesu said.

By the time the group executioners got back to the village, Kekoyi had committed suicide.

XXII

It was on the eve of Yesu's thirty-third birthday that the Star of Destiny led Yesu and his followers to Betu-Akara, his place of birth. They arrived there early in the morning of his birthday. As had become their tradition over the past three years, Aken announced their arrival in the village with his drum. People came out of their homes to welcome them. Yesu was unusually silent as they arrived his village. He did not speak much, neither did his crack his unending jokes. He appeared to be in deep thoughts.

They moved to the village square as people followed and danced to Aken's drum. By midday, almost all the villagers had come to see them and to hear the tales of their travels and their message. The elders took their seats under a tree and drank palm-wine. All the women were clad in their best attires, and those with children had also dressed them in their best attires. It had been a very long time since Betu-Akara had seen strangers from another land. They were all curious to hear these strangers. A big feast was prepared for them.
Tradition demanded that all strangers introduced themselves to the assembly before they launched

into their tales and the purpose of their journey. This introduction demanded the recital of lineage. This meant that the person would mention his village of origin, his name, the names of his father and mother as well as the names of the grandparents.

One by one, the followers of Yesu introduced themselves to the gathering and in the course of their narration mentioned how they had met Yesu, their Master. As a natural speaker, Miroke spoke for long and praised their Master. He told them of his experience with Yesu on the Lake of Adagun and of many wonders that he had done in the past three years that he had known him. All the villagers looked with awe at Yesu, who was quiet and appeared to be troubled.

When it was Yesu's turn to speak, he got up slowly, looked up to the sky and said, "I am Yesu, the Son of Most High Olodumare!" Then he sat down. The people wanted more, but Yesu resolutely refused. Aken ended the introduction with his drum. It was time to eat and drink.

It was a big feast. People ate and drank. After food, more kegs of palm-wine were brought out.

Yesu drank very little, but his followers, except Yonda, drank with abandon with the elders. The elders wanted to know more about Yesu, so they plied the followers with plenty of wine. Soon, some of them were tipsy. The elders pulled aside the youngest of his followers, gave him more wine and asked him, "Tell us more about your Master. We intend to give him land for him to make his home among us."

"My Master does not need land. He does not need a house."

"Ok. But you would like to have land and a house if possible. We can give you and give you money to build."

"Really! I don't want the land or the house. Just give me money."

"Ok. Here is money. We can give you more if you want!"

"Yes! What do you want to know about him?"

"Very simple things. Unlike all of you, he did not tell us the names of his father and mother and his village of birth."

The follower laughed and said, "Is that all? There is nothing special about that."

"Indeed! Tell us!"

"I once overheard that he was born here in Betu-Akara. His father was Yiofikun and the mother was Murewa. She has two other mothers, Abike and Rojoyin."

The elders looked at each other. It dawned on them that this was the boy The Regulators had condemned to death many years ago. Bound by the curse of The Regulators, they knew they had to kill him. They thanked the follower and sent him back to the group to continue his merriment.

Yesu saw him and beckoned to him.

"Why did you do that? How much did they give you? You have given me away to be killed? Why?"

"No, Master. Emmm….they just wanted to know about your parents! I am sorry!"

"Too late! Here they come!"

The elders had mobilized the youth to seize Yesu. As they chanted war song, the people, including the followers of Yesu scrambled away in fear from the centre of the village square and moved to the periphery. Yesu stood alone, calm, his head bent. He did not struggle when they seized him. They quickly de-robed him and started hitting him with their sticks. They held him fast.

Silence befell the compound as The Regulators with their *Atokun* marched into the village square.

The young men holding Yesu left him and moved back. The Regulators encircled him. They mumbled among themselves and the Atokun relayed their discussion in loud voice.

"This is the man grown out of the baby boy that was condemned to death thirty-three years ago. He was born after six months of marriage and he caused the death and disappearance of our brave hunters when they went into the bush to look for him and his parents. The sentence of The Regulators who have since gone to join their ancestors was that he should be put to cruel death if he ever set his foot on this land. We must carry out the sentence so that the souls of the departed Regulators could rest in peace and that our land may be cleansed from the evil this person put on our land thirty-three years ago." The people shouted, "Yes! Yes! Kill him! Put him to death!"

The Atokun continued, "This shall be his mode of death:
His body shall be rubbed with honey.
He will be taken to the red ant infected acacia tree at the edge of the village.
His hands shall be tied to the branches, his legs tied to the trunk of the tree.

Seven young men and seven hunters shall hit him with their sticks till he dies.
His body shall be left on the tree for the ants, birds, rats and other animals.
Seven hunters shall guard the body day and night for the next twenty-one days!"

After the pronouncement, The Regulators marched out of the square.

The people, who had been feasting with him and his followers just a few hours before started chanting,
"Kill him! Kill him! Kill him!" His followers scampered for safety.
The appointed fourteen executioners rubbed honey on his body and started beating him with their sticks as they dragged him out of the village to the tree. He was already unconscious by the time they got him to the foot of the tree. Smelling honey, the giant red ants attacked Yesu's body as the men tied ropes on each his arms. Done, they threw the ropes up the branches and each side of the tree and hauled up the body and secured the ropes on the branches. They could hear the shoulder bones cracking as they hauled him up. After this, they tied his feet together before securing them with a

rope around the trunk of the tree. After this, they took up their sticks and hit him all over the body and head hundreds of times. It was sunset by the time they finished killing him. He was killed on his thirty-third birthday.

Back in the village square, where people were singing and dancing to celebrate the capture and killing of Yesu, one of the villagers apprehended Miroke as he tried to sneak out.
"I remember you! You are one of his followers!"
"Are you drunk? That is not true. I am not."
"But you are dressed like him!"
"Man, watch your wine. You have been drinking too much!"
Miroke rapidly made his way out of the village square to seek out the other followers. He found them huddled together under a tree in the bush at a distance from the village. Yonda was not there, and he feared for her life.
Soon, Yonda arrived, furious at the other followers.
"Where have you been?" Miroke asked.
"I went there with him. I was there as they beat him to death. I saw everything! He was almost dead before they hung him on the tree. They beat

him to death. Then I returned to the village square where I collected his robe from some gamblers."

"You went there? You saw everything?"

"Yes! And you, Miroke? I saw and heard you when one person asked if you were one of his followers. Remember what you said? And you slithered away like a snake."

"Shhhh….don't let the others hear you!" He pleaded.

"I am angry at all of you. You are all cowards! You all ran away when he needed you the most!" She cried.

"There was nothing we could do! You saw that too!"

She abruptly sat on a stone and started wailing. The other followers also broke into tears. The follower who had divulged information about Yesu was nowhere to be found. His body, half-eaten by red ants and rats was found the following day.

It was a most difficult night for Yesu's followers. When they looked up in the pitch-dark sky, the star of Destiny was no longer there, neither were the other usual ones. The night was so unusually dark that they could not even see each other. They were caught between the fatigue of the day and deep grief. They dozed fitfully and woke up with a start at any little sound. Yonda did not sleep.

Fearing for their lives, the followers did not venture out the next day. Yonda was restless. She could not go anywhere. She neither ate not drank. She hoped that she could sneak out in the night to go to the execution place. However, it was the night of *Oro*, when only the initiates could come out and women were forbidden at the pain of death to set eyes on the human-made apparition. She waited in the dark until about daybreak when the *Oro* ceremony would have ended and then set out.

She went directly to where Yesu was executed the evening of the day before. She saw the hunters who guarded the body, well asleep, she sidestepped them and went directly to the tree. She regretted she no longer had any *champaca* oil. She so much would have loved to rub the oil on his body and his wounds.

When she got to the tree, the body was not there. She looked frantically around. All the ropes with which they had tied him to the tree laid at the foot of the tree! She suppressed a shout. She groped on the soil in the surrounding bush to see if he was there. She was confused.

Jumping over the hunters who were still fast asleep, she ran very fast to where the other followers were. Panting, she informed Miroke what she had seen.
"He is no longer there! They have taken our Master! And I have no idea where he has been taken! Yonda cried.

All Yesu's followers got up and ran after Yonda who had started running again to the site of the execution. Soon, Aken and a disciple called Fajonu outran her and reached the execution tree. Miroke and the others trailed along. When they got to the execution place, hhey saw the hunters still fast asleep.

They looked around but did not find any traces of the body in the bush. The ropes with which he had been tied were neatly folded at the foot of the tree. They found heaps of dead red ants around the tree too.

After they had satisfied themselves that the body was not anywhere close to the execution place,

Miroke asked everyone to return to where they were camped outside the village. Yonda cried all along the way asking Miroke repeatedly, "Where have they taken my Master?"

It was Yonda that first saw him in their camp seated on a stone, chewing a small stick. He was dressed in white. She ran to Yesu and he hugged her.

"My Lord!" She gasped.

Yesu gave his characteristic smile and said, "Welcome Yonda, the true servant of Olodumare!"

"Hey! Master! How did you get here? They killed you day before yesterday!" Miroke said from a distance.

Yesu smiled and said, "They killed the body but not the spirit. No one can kill the spirit of Olodumare that lives in every one of us!"

"Are you really our Master?"

"Yes!"

"Ok. Tell me the name of my last wife before I abandoned them all to follow you""

"Miroke! I know many things. Even in the agony of death on that cursed tree, I heard when you told one of the villagers that you were not one of my followers! You denied me!"

Miroke, head bowed and shedding tears, knelt, and said, "Master, please forgive me!"

Yesu waved to him to get up and said, "No problems Miroke. I forgave you before it happened!"

Miroke and the other followers rushed towards him. He stretched out his hand and told them not to move too close as his wounds were still raw and getting smelly.

"Who cares about smelly wounds?" Miroke cried. They mobbed him.

In their absence, he had prepared breakfast. No one had any idea where he got the food and the ingredients from and no one asked. It was a meal of yams and vegetables. They sat in a circle on the damp earth.

"This meal is the symbol of your communion with me. Do this often among yourselves. And remember me whenever you do it!" Yesu said.

"Master! What does this mean? To remember you? How? You are here with us. We are here with you!" Miroke said in exasperation. He did not want Yesu to leave them ever again.

"Miroke! Listen to me! You are now the leader. I will inspire and guide you in your new responsibilities! Now! Eat the yam and the vegetables. The yam represents my body!"

"Your body? How?" Fajonu asked. He moved closer to Yesu and asked to sit on his left side. Yonda, with her head on Yesu's shoulders was seated on his right.

"Yes! My body! Do this sharing of food in remembrance of me!"

"But Master, we are not cannibals! Why did you say the yam represents your body? I don't want to imagine eating your flesh!"

"Do it, so that I can live in you. You will be able to do everything that you saw me do, and even more!"

They solemnly shared the yam and ate the vegetables.

He took a small keg of palm-wine, drank from it and passed it to the followers to drink. He said, "that is my blood. Whenever you are together, do this sharing of palm-wine or any other liquid in my remembrance. My spirit will live in you."

"But Master, this is getting strange. I have never heard you speak like this since I have known you. You have always talked in simple language. What is this story of body and blood and remembrance?"

"My dear Miroke, you know some things, but you do not know everything. But you will understand with time."

The followers were downcast. Yesu stood up and brought a pot of water. He knelt before Yonda and washed her feet. He washed the feet of each of the followers. When done, he said, "your feet are cleansed and ready to carry you to all the corners of the world." The followers started to cry.

"Pack your things. Hurry! We do not have much time left."

Yesu led the way through the bush in the direction of River Monilo. When they reached the banks, they moved in the direction of a big tree that cast its huge dark shadow on the River. A long canoe was moored to the tree. Under the tree, stood a man in white billowing robes with a staff in his hand.

Yesu signalled to his followers to stop at a distance as he walked towards the man. The man bowed as Yesu reached him. He gestured with his hand towards the canoe. He held the canoe steady and Yesu climbed into it and went to sit in front.

He then climbed in, sat at the back, and with two long oars steered the canoe to the middle of the river and then into the horizon.